THOUGHTWORLD
Terry Greenhough

NEW ENGLISH LIBRARY/TIMES MIRROR

First published in Great Britain by
New English Library in 1977
© by Terry Greenhough, 1977

First NEL Paperback edition
November 1978

NEL Books are published by
New English Library Limited from
Barnard's Inn, Holborn,
London EC1N 2JR
Made and printed in Great Britain by
Hunt Barnard Printing Ltd,
Aylesbury, Bucks

45003640 5

THOUGHTWORLD

Chapter One

Inside Thoughtworld, Dizzy Derek changed summer into winter. He removed the leaves, the blue sky and bright flowers. In their place he put snow-covered skeletal trees, a howling blizzard and bleak white hills. He was childishly pleased with the transformation.

Idly he glanced at the date-panel: 5–4–245 – Day 5, Fourmonth, Year of the Confederation 245. Wasn't it today that the new Director should arrive? Or should it have been yesterday? No, because he hadn't come yet. It must be today, then. Perhaps.

Dizzy Derek didn't really know and didn't really care. Directors drifted in and out in endless procession, haughtily in, glumly out, at the whim of the financial backers of Thoughtworld. So what? Another one wouldn't make much difference. If he left Derek alone, fine. And even if he didn't, it wouldn't worry Derek.

Halfway between ceiling and floor, Derek went to sleep.

'What do you think he'll be like?' asked Arkon Vitch, several rooms away. He nodded to the outer vastness from which the Director would ship-in. Space waited in the screens as Vitch and Silver waited in Communications.

'Does it matter? There's some good, some bad, some nothing.' Silver spoke indifferently through her mask. Methane and ammonia flowed into her lungs with her steady breathing, keeping her alive. 'I'm not bothered, Ark.'

Tubes curled from the air-pack on her back. The mask hid much of her attractive face. Her curvaceous body glittered – shiny, scaly, silver. She stood only 5ft tall, human in shape but not in classification. Short iridescent hair framed the sheen of her delicate features. Vitch considered her the most beautiful creature in Thoughtworld or anywhere else. He wanted to kiss her, but without the mask she'd die. A gasping influx of oxygen and she'd wriggle out her life in his arms, flap like a stranded fish – scales flashing, an agonised frenzy, death. He could only gaze at her in open admiration.

She glanced upwards, contemplated eleven dead men – eleven corpses, thirty-three years old, grisly leftovers from the time when multiple destruction had hit Thoughtworld: Day 8, Fourmonth, YC 212. The bodies hadn't been found. They were still concealed in the crust, perhaps occasionally within touching-distance. The idea sent a tremor of fascinated horror through her.

Next to the visiplate, a light blinked for attention. 'Oho! The new lamb for eventual slaughter?' Arkon wondered how long the latest Director would last.

A face appeared on the plate, above a uniform, backed by the inside of a vessel. The comm-officer looked young, fresh, eager. Stiffly he recited the correct identification letters. 'THEEO?' He didn't elaborate on what they signified. An adjacent screen showed a collection of dots: part of Confed Squadron 17, in precise formation, escorting the civilian liner carrying the expected *Sciri* (Professor) Pertra. 'Artificial planet Theeo, please acknowledge.'

Characteristically, Arkon did. 'This is Thoughtworld.'

'Huh?' The operator was obviously raw. 'Artificial planet Theeo, please ack — '

'This is Thoughtworld,' Arkon interrupted the mechanically repeated request. 'Theeo to you; Thoughtworld to us.' Theeo's staff never responded to the proper title. It was a point of honour, a display of independence. But they weren't independent and they knew it. They hovered on the brink of the most intellectual breakthrough of all time – as amazing as the shattering Tynar's Hypothesis – but they weren't independent. Smiling, Arkon Vitch stressed stubbornly, '*Thoughtworld* acknowledging.'

'Good enough. Prepare to receive the replacement Director, Sciri Pertra. We'll be with you inside two minutes.'

6

'Okay.' Arkon watched the screen go blank, felt a feather-light touch on his arm: Silver's slim hand. He stared at the neighbouring scanner. The dots were enlarging swiftly. Behind them hung the yellow glare of distant 17/LS6, the nearest star. New Athens wasn't visible.

Tiny toes twisted nervously inside Silver's mag-boots. Although she wasn't greatly concerned over the imminent arrival, she sensed a slight apprehension. She tried to smother it but couldn't. Jewel-like eyes narrowed under the rainbow-blaze of perfumed hair.

Sciri Pertra, Professor Pertra: yet another Director for Theeo, the most recent in a long line. Would he keep to himself and let the staff get on with their work unmolested? She hoped so. Or would he be forever prying and prodding, jabbering about deadlines, fretting over schedules? That sort of approach to the job she didn't like, yet she under-stood it and could almost sympathise with those who had the precarious task of managing Thoughtworld.

Something continually prodded *them*: a lurking, vicious, hydra-headed monster called the Thirteen – a monster whose attacks were intensified and complicated by the intricacy of interworld and internation politics. It had a disturbing habit of reminding Theeo who paid the bills and the salaries. It snapped angrily at the throats of Directors, worrying them. Sometimes it bit them clear out of a job. Thirteen planets had promoted Thoughtworld. Thirteen planets meant a lot of vested interests. Often the vested interests grew impatient and governments saw fit to apply pressure. They'd driven many a Director to resignation and one to suicide.

'Just so long as he sticks to administration, Ark; I don't mind then.' He noticed her peculiar inflexion, a word-slurring worsened by the mask. That mask! So vital to her, so infuriating to him. Here in Communications, powerful fans circulated oxygenated air. In Silver's own private part of Thoughtworld they whirled poisonous methane and ammonia. To go there, Vitch had to mask-up before passing through the lock.

Deftly he unbuckled his mag-boots. A gentle push and he floated serenely to the ceiling, stayed on it a moment. Then he flicked himself expertly down again and snatched a handhold. Dozens of them met his eyes as he buckled the boots: on walls, ceiling, floor. They were everywhere in Thoughtworld, firm grips set into strong but lightweight plastic. Metal walkways sliced all surfaces, for booted loco-motion whenever necessary. Mostly, people sailed.

Silver and Arkon glanced at the screen as Squadron 17's ship-specks englobed Theeo. The commercial vessel peeled off and approached slowly. Twelve squadron ships formed a protective funnel around it, the open end to Thought-world.

'Look at that, Silver! The military mind! A perfect en-globement, a cone pouring us a Director inwards, precautions and precision on every hand. And all quite unnecessary! Still, I imagine somebody's having fun giving the orders.'

'Playing games, Ark.' Neither Silver nor Arkon had any time for military discipline. Theirs were potent minds and their own willpower alone held them on course. They kicked back violently at any external urging – a trait shared by almost everyone who worked in Theeo, a characteristic nourished with pride: the pride of being privileged, different, in a class apart, a Thoughtworlder!

The civilian ship flamed to a halt in space. Nothing ever touched down on small hollow Theeo. From the hull a slender cylinder drove out, connecting silently with an on-the-surface embarkation hatch after a few minutes of skilful manoeuvring. Vitch marvelled at the dexterity of the pilot, but frowned as he saw the vessel's identification. The code gave its home base as Hope, one of thirteen planets respon-sible for Theeo's existence. Perturbed, he turned to Silver. 'They've never appointed their lambs from any of the Thirteen before.' He didn't add his own cynical opinion, that it was less troublesome to terminate abruptly the ser-vices of an outsider. 'Still, if this Sciri Pertra *is* from Hope, he might be a welcome change. An individual who's come up through ability and made them alter their policy.' Then he thought of the opposite side of the coin: or a piece of putty, a puppet, pliable!

Without noise, the connecting tube withdrew. The Director was inside.

*

'Might as well go to have a look,' Dizzy Derek said, then answered himself amicably: 'I agree.' There was no one else in the room. He frequently talked to himself, but nobody took much notice. They didn't take much notice of him whatever he did. Sometimes they showed amusement at his more foolish phases, his more stupid phrases. They played harmless little tricks on him and he laughed as loudly as anyone at the outcome. Occasionally a prankster went a tiny bit too far and something hard flashed through Derek's easy-going façade. But folks usually ignored him.

He changed winter back into summer and left at a brisk float.

His hand sought a grip, and it propelled him along, head-first and horizontal. Three times his fingers curled around tough protuberances as he sailed in the direction of Communications.

He grinned as he flew. Arkon the Solemn would be in Communications, tending the scanners. Silver the Beautiful wouldn't be far away, not if Arkon was there!

Grabbing and drifting, Dizzy Derek pondered. Thought-world boasted no technicians. Not that it needed many. Practically everything was in the control of machines: heating, lighting, repairs and food-preparation. Robots were always racing down the walkways, tidying bedrooms, cleaning lavatories, polishing away madly with all the mindless indefatigability of steel cretins.

'Maids in metal,' muttered Derek, to nobody.

A few jobs required real live flesh and blood. Someone had to check the screens regularly. Arkon saw to it, uncomplainingly. 'He thinks I'm incompetent,' mused Derek, admitting the truth of it. He got on well with Arkon; he got on well with nearly everyone, but he never forgot those who went too far!

With a shrewdness to which he wouldn't have dreamed of confessing, he realised why Communications had been located down here and nowhere else. Because down here just happened to be A-block, and A-block contained the cream of Thoughtworld, the best brains. And some fool just happened to consider it a good idea to leave a tedious

9

task to the best brains, to stop their egos swelling beyond bounds.

'They're trying to keep us down-to-earth,' Derek told himself. 'Which is exactly what Thoughtworld was designed *not* to do!' He shook his head in wordless compassion for all people more idiotic than he.

As graceful as a bird, he rode air through the rooms and corridors of A-block – past Silver's quarters with its lethal atmosphere, past huge seldom-entered chambers where machines clicked incessantly. Whenever a closed exit panel confronted him, he pressed the release button and said, 'Open, Theodore!' Then he dived through, chuckling. In Theeo, all doors were called Theodore – a habit started by Derek. Several more grabs and Derek hovered outside Communications, steadying himself. Smoothly he glided to the floor, steering for a pair of mag-boots. They lined all walks at intervals, to be used when required. He didn't like wearing them, but Arkon tended to get upset if bodies whirled around him as he concentrated on the screens.

A boot was fought on to each foot and Derek stood on the walkway. To either side of the metal, a plastic floor met plastic walls which met a plastic ceiling. Derek shuffled off slowly, as awkward in the boots as he was expert without them. Arkon, Silver, Cleo Rosa, even bloated old Gormal could manage perfectly well in boots, and could actually pick one foot up after the other and progress properly and unrestricted.

Dizzy Derek shuffled, sliding his feet along the steel. He didn't dare lift either. Once, early on, he'd made the mistake of slithering off on to the plastic and whoosh! he was airborne. He'd been a floater ever since, a reluctant walker.

He entered Communications. Silver and Arkon turned, speaking together. 'Hi, Dizzy.' They said it affably, without stifled or overt laughter.

It didn't worry Derek to be addressed as Dizzy. He thought: 'Well, I am, aren't I?' and smiled his best vacant smile. Unsteadily he crossed to the screen. 'He's here?'

'Almost'. Vitch waved a large hand at the image. The connection cylinder had retracted. The non-military ship was turning sluggishly. Squadron 17 had regrouped and presently, space yawned empty except for sun 17/LS6. New Athens, its only inhabited planet, wasn't visible. 'Yes, he's almost here, Dizzy. A Hope-type, probably. If that gives *us* cause to hope!'

Perfume wafted; Silver's colourful hair danced as her head jerked to Arkon. 'Let's not prejudge him, Ark.' She felt a little sorry for the Director as she pictured him clambering down the Hole: hand over hand, dragging himself cautiously 'downwards' in no-grav inside a shaft joining Thoughtworld's surface to its interior. Then the lock at the bottom would disgorge him here in Communications.

She wondered what he'd be like, what kind of supervisor. And what sort of creature was he, what species? He must be an oxygen-breather, because there'd been no instructions about air change. Apart from that, all she knew was his title and name: Sciri Pertra. It told her hardly anything.

A buzz and the lock door slid across. A suited cumbersome figure trundled out. His boots held him to the walkway while he stood breathing heavily. Sciri Pertra had arrived.

He opened with a laugh aimed at himself, brittle-sounding through the visor. 'Obviously a poor learner on the no-grav course.' His voice was deep, the accent no clue to his race. Clumsily he unsuited and revealed himself: a very tall and stout biped, greyish face and fat belly. 'Greetings to you all! This is Sciri Pertra, your . . . Director.' He seemed embarrassed at mentioning his position of authority.

Vitch performed perfunctory introductions, and Pertra shook hands all round. His own huge paw dwarfed even Arkon's, utterly engulfed Silver's and squeezed firmly against Dizzy's slack grip. Derek smiled his vacant smile again. 'I've forgot the welcome speech.'

'Ah, please, no speeches for this one!' Pertra paused, took a few tentative steps and proved himself more adept than Derek in mag-boots. 'Yet all of you of A-block are not here?'

'No,' Vitch answered. 'Gormal's in his tank and Cleo Rosa's in Think. You want them fetched?'

'But no, I thank you! No inconvenience for them on my account.' He looked around, noticing the walks and handholds. 'Like a baby child I have much to learn. To propel myself.'

11

'You'll get used to it,' Arkon said, and thought: 'If they give you time!' Aloud, he continued, 'Not the safest of jobs you've dropped into, you know. Thirty-two years since Thoughtworld started. Twenty-one Directors. That's an average of ...'

'Ah, but my arithmetic is equal to it, my friend. Now, if someone would be so kind as to show me to my office and quarters ...'

At a nod from Arkon, Derek offered. They left together, an experienced shuffler and a fairly capable beginner. Silver's eyes flashed a question and Arkon replied, 'He's okay, I suppose. Friendly. Pleasant. But too soft. He won't last a month!'

Chapter Two

Two guns spewed hot death and a rebel died. The two Enforcement men approached the corpse, poked it with large boots. It didn't move. Dead eyes gazed sightlessly at the autumn sky above New Athens.

Crumpled and torn, the body stained the street with a spreading pool of red.

'One less,' the first killer said flatly.

'Aye.' The second man nursed his chatter-gun, slipping it into its holster and blessing its quiet action. 'He had it coming. We'd no choice.'

Somehow you didn't feel quite so responsible for a killing when you could scarcely hear it done. With a chatter-gun, death hit very quietly; like ramming a knife in a rebel's back – all you heard, if anything, was a gurgle. And even then, *you* hadn't broken the silence; *he* had. It made a difference.

Four parted curtains revealed curious eyes. Otherwise the street minded its own business. The city of Attica, capital of New Athens, chose not to notice most of the rebels shot down in its open spaces and dark holes.

There weren't many rebels anyway, and the chatter-guns were so *silent*. A noise? Maybe. Or maybe not. Perhaps the wind whispering.

'That's what I said. Dead.' A voice rasped into a radio, giving an exact location. 'It wants shifting. It's messing the road up.' A quick and efficient cleaning detail would be along soon. A few bloodspots might remain, but Attica had a high rainfall. No trace! With the body in an unmarked grave.

A hand stroked a holster. There was now one rebel less to

threaten Prime Minister Lundren's regime. But what about the rest of them? They'd be in well-concealed hideaways somewhere, waiting and waiting. For what? For the day when there'd be enough of them to swarm up out of their ratholes and attempt what Lev Merrin had tried in 238.

The Enforcement man smirked, thinking: 'Hurray the day! It'll take plenty of you to topple Lundren. Men as big as him don't topple easily!'

Then he said aloud, 'Come on, we've done our bit.' But somehow he didn't feel proud. The killing hadn't elated him; it had sickened him. Something foul-tasting stuck in his throat and crawled around in his stomach. Mentally, he endeavoured to console himself: 'It's only a job, that's all. Somebody's got to ferret them out. If it wasn't me, it'd be . . . ' He left off, glancing down. Christ, the corpse didn't look like a rebel! Just a youngster, really. Alien, yes, but what of it? Not all the rebels were alien. Not all the Enforcement people were human. It wasn't a racial problem. What was it, then? Social? Probably. Political? Definitely!

That was it: politics. A minority of the population of New Athens wanted Lundren out. Lundren wanted Lundren in. It was as simple as that, and as difficult! Because men as big as Joab Lundren didn't topple easily. They clung to their positions tenaciously, ruthlessly if necessary. According to some of the rumours that went the rounds, Joab Lundren could be as ruthless as death itself. He was reckoned to have his share of innocent blood on his hands and more besides. But you couldn't prove it. When a man reached the top of the tree, he usually had sufficient power to cover up all the chopping and hacking he'd done on the way up. You couldn't accuse him either. You took a risk listening to the rumour-whisperers, a greater risk if you were actually doing the whispering. To so much as admit you'd heard there *were* rumours was a chancy business, too.

The Enforcement man's memory flickered back to Merrin's doomed insurgence in 238. He hadn't stood the slightest chance. All the same, he'd tried. You had to admire him. He'd tried. He wouldn't try again. An unmarked grave held the pieces.

But somebody would rise again, one day. And what chance

14

did *they* stand? Not much. There'd been no Enforcement Agency in 238, no weapons on Lundren's side. Then, New Athens had truly been what Lundren so often proclaimed it: Peace Planet – on the surface, at least. Until Merrin struck, briefly and bloodily.

Today the EA was as strong as Joab could make it, which meant very strong. And quiet. Undercover. The government didn't recognise it officially; it just paid wages to certain people at certain times for doing certain things which, according to the government, didn't need to be done.

Walking down the street, one of the Enforcement men thought of the strangeness of his position. He was part of the planet's best-kept secret, a member of a force not known offworld, and he walked down a street in full view armed. On Peace Planet.

Someday the secret would escape. The Confed would hear of it. Somebody who was in accord with Lundren would nevertheless open his mouth and say something he'd immediately regret. And then . . .

Grey with dusk, a window framed a head grey with age. Joab Lundren stared up at the darkening sky: several tiny specks, distant suns, glinting in the evening. In the Confederation's sparsely starred Sector 17, night came as a blackness unrelieved except for a handful of scattered light points, faint and flickering. Theeo was too small and far away to be seen.

Lundren pulled down the curtain, switched on the light and seated himself behind a desk littered with papers. His broad shoulders bowed as he bent to work. The weight of years and responsibility told on him. He felt sorry for himself. He was Prime Minister of New Athens and he still couldn't rest content, say applaudingly to his reflection in the mirror, 'You had an ambition, a dream. You've fulfilled it. Sleep well, old man.'

The demon of ambition drove him even now. It pushed him while death pulled and mocked. He knew he couldn't hope for more than a decade or two. It didn't seem much.

It wasn't enough. His plans went beyond twenty years, but almost certainly his body wouldn't.

So many worries! The rebels, the strain of letting an entire world in on a secret, yet at the same time ensuring that all lips likely to reveal it were closed forever. The business of the Thirteen to attend to: conferences, arguments over money, keeping an eye on Theeo.

He pronounced solemn silent anathema on Theeo's personnel. Why did they have to be so obstinate, so unruly, so undisciplined? Complacently referring to their place of work as Thoughtworld, for instance, where was the sense in that? The planet was Theeo. Why call it anything else?

Lundren thumped the desk angrily, and thought: 'I made Theeo! It's mine! Tynar gets all the credit, though, and what did he do? Dreamed up the wretched Hypothesis – with my help, which everyone forgets – and then died in a blaze of fame. And so for me, why, I only fought a dozen fronts at once to make Tynar's Hypothesis a concrete practicable reality! I turned an abstraction into solid form. I *made* Theeo!'

It was partly true.

He banged a bell viciously and an assistant hurried in: a tried and trusted young man who knew when to bow, when to scrape, when to speak. And, most important of all, when not to. 'Sir?'

Lundren passed across a list of names. 'Scrub this lot. Known dissidents and possible talkers. Get the EA on it tonight.' It was unfortunate: fifty murders before morning. But it couldn't be helped. He'd built Peace Planet from nothing and it had a reputation to be maintained. With the good name of a good planet to be upheld, a mere fifty people or so now and then couldn't be allowed to matter. Lundren couldn't afford scruples.

He thought irritably: 'The EA's necessary!' Which was correct, since 238. Merrin had been a nuisance at the time and death hadn't ended his threat. His name was still whispered in cellars and remote houses all over New Athens. His followers constituted more than a nuisance. They were a positive menace to the planet's stability and Joab Lundren's life.

'Suffer not a menace to live,' he paraphrased coldly, and considered it ample justification. Yet a little corner of his mind wouldn't stay quiet. It muttered insidiously, 'These so-called rebels aren't *bad*. They just have different opinions to yours. That's not sufficient cause for wholesale murder . . . ' But he refused to listen to it any more. He forced his brain to think of other things – things he'd done, things he'd said, the considerable influence he'd had in the shaping of the Confed. It titillated his vanity to look back.

The Conference of Hope, in 209: thirteen worlds had met to enquire into the feasibility of sponsoring a non-natural planetoid answering the requirements of Tynar's Hypothesis. Lundren remembered anxious days of discussion, wrangling and invective. Almost single-handed he'd battled Theeo into being. He'd organised designers, construction workers and the collection of funds. He'd sat with a committee set up to decide on the number and qualifications of Theeo's staff. He'd made a world to test the Hypothesis. And yet the Confed called Tynar the Father of Thoughtworld!

The colonisation of New Athens, in 197: Lundren himself had led the dissatisfied multitude, a motley herd seeking a place where they could live their lives as they wished. They'd settled in New Athens, eleven species in all, and later there'd been a colossal immigration of similar thinkers: searchers after peace, members of the anti-war factions, the lonely and the malcontents.

'I moulded them,' Lundren thought smugly. 'I formed their government, this democratic system of ours – democratic in so far as the populace thinks it rules! I made New Athens! The world with no armed forces except the secret pest controllers, the vermin chasers. Peace Planet. It has never been attacked, and never will be. The world of the intelligentsia, the acclaimed artists, the misguided altruists. I made it! Who's the Father of Peace Planet, Tynar? Not you!'

But Lundren knew Peace Planet wasn't so peaceful nowadays.

Gormal wallowed in his tank, ruminating. Dirty black water

foamed as he flopped his enormous body about. Strengthened glass kept the water inside the tank, a cube 10 yd on a side.

He mused happily on the 1000 cu yd of mucky liquid surrounding him, remembering the vast oceans of home: hundreds of miles deep, a boiling thunder of chaotic currents above a slimy bed of luxurious clinging ooze. By comparison, the tank wasn't much. Still, it was something; somewhere to escape to whenever he wanted to relax and do some private extra-schedule thinking.

What about the new Director? Hadn't seen him yet. He'd been here a full day, so perhaps it was time to make his acquaintance. No, why bother? Thoughtworlders often saw more than enough of their Directors as things stood.

Across Gormal's brilliant mind ran memories of folders with various official stamps on them: 'Top priority', 'urgent', 'very urgent'. And a stream of separate Directors rushing about, frantically demanding whether you'd dealt with them all. Courtesy, Gormal decided. For the sake of politeness, he'd better present himself, get the other's measure. There was always a slim chance of his being a decent supervisor, the sort who hardly ever came out of his office; a straightforward administrator, who realised people could work far more efficiently without others constantly harassing them.

Gormal fumbled through the wet murk, knocking down a switch. Noisily the emptying mechanism sucked the water out. Nozzles entered, spraying the glass and the grotesque occupant. Slime fell off and was swallowed. He stood there a moment, monstrous and naked. Then he touched another switch and the front section of the tank opened. He fumbled out into weightlessness and shook himself. Later, robots would buzz along and pick globules of moisture from the air.

Gormal went to find the Director.

Meanwhile, the Director himself was indicating his own chest. He looked up at the girl before him. 'This is Sciri Pertra. Professor Pertra. Your . . . Director.' Again embarrassment trembled in his voice. He stared at the ice fields, bewildered. 'You'll be Cleo Rosa?'

'Until I die.' She grinned prettily. Her lithe body hung in mid-air, tiny and lovely, similar to Silver's in size and contour, but human. Ebon hair billowed in static waves around a dark oval face. Eyes black and deep as infinity drifted an appraising gaze lazily over Pertra. The scrutiny ended and the laziness vanished. Everything about Cleo Rosa now suggested vibrant vitality, a sparkling intensity caged in the frame of a seductive houri. 'Pleased to meet you, Sciri Pertra.'

'Just Pertra, if you would,' he requested diffidently. 'A name is sufficient for this one. The title makes him feel old and venerable. He's neither. And as for meeting you, well, I'll say hello from down here, if you don't mind. It doesn't look safe up there and I'm not ready to start experimenting yet.'

Cleo Rosa smiled with all the warm enchantment of antique Asia-Terra. This Pertra was pleasantly different. Usually a new Thoughtworld boss blasted in with banners waving, puffed out with assumed self-importance. Pertra had humility. She liked him. 'Found your way around yet?'

'By no means. Only around some of A-block. The rest I'll leave.' He contemplated the other staffed places in Theeo: the student-wings where promising youngsters learned Thoughtworld techniques, the smaller blocks in which less-gifted people did less-important work. He'd decided not to visit them, in case the lower echelons considered him guilty of condescension. 'I'll stay in A. I'd be obliged if you could pass the word on: my office is always open for anyone, any time.'

'Sure.' She hoped he'd last but doubted it. With a suddenness that surprised him, she obliterated the desolate polar wastes in the room. Her mood had been slightly frosty, but he'd changed it. India blossomed, a circumambient vista from light-years distant, centuries ago. Mysticism painted god-colours on squalor. Music wailed, a haunting background, inaudible yet somehow there.

'Remarkable!' he congratulated. 'This Pertra wishes he could do that.'

'No chance, I'm afraid. It's only for us Thinkers, not you . . . ' She stopped short, regret pulsing in a crimson flood beneath the sombre beauty of her cheeks. 'Sorry. I didn't mean anything by that.'

19

He dismissed it with a genuine smile, grey but reassuring. 'Forget it. We can't all reach the heights. I'm glad to have got to Theeo in any capacity.'

'Even the highest?'

Pertra laughed. 'Highest? In salary and authority, yes. But not in pure intellect. I'm aware of my uses. Also my shortcomings. If one admits these, he can do much worse.'

'And very little better. I see your philosophy matches that which was a part of me before I was born.'

'You please me, Cleo Rosa. Our spirits harmonise. Where I was born, on a world now within the Benlhaut Empire . . . '

She twisted abruptly in nothingness, facing him like a lovely lethal arrow of flesh, frowning. 'The Benlhaut Empire? You aren't . . . ?'

'No, no,' he broke in gently. 'I'm as loyal to the Confederation as anybody. Since I was ten, Hope is my planet and owns my allegiance. It's merely that the world where I lived as a child, then free and autonomous, was later swallowed by the voracious mouth of the Emperor. Bloodlessly, though, and not altogether to its detriment. I sympathise with Benlhaut up to a point. Its alien ruler and his incomprehensible ethics may strike us as tyrannical, yet not every fish in the Imperial pool has cancerous scales.'

'You think there'll be war?'

'In these days of colossal destruction potential? But no! Politicians love to make threats and meaningless gestures; it's a universal disease from which most of them suffer. Although surely not even they desire so much death!'

'Optimist,' said Cleo Rosa. Then she recollected an adage from antiquity and quoted it: 'Optimism is often precious but costs nothing, yet when it is seen to have been misplaced, it exacts a terrible price indeed!'

A tremendous amount of paperwork covered Pertra's desk: requests for a Thinker to sort out this problem, demands for a Thinker to sort out that one, a miscellany ranging from polite applications to unequivocal orders, the accumulated backlog of the interregnum, he realised. Not sure where to begin, he flicked through forms at random. 'Lords of Void,' he cursed inwardly, 'not even a secretary to help!' It looked like being a long haul to so much as catch up to the point at which his predecessor had broken off, or been broken off! Twenty-one Directors in thirty-two years? No, it definitely wasn't the most secure post in the Confed.

He selected a paper, pulled it from under the spring clip that held it to the desk. Fingers fumbled and it floated away in no-grav. Its action reminded him to tighten the straps that kept him in his seat. He glanced at the office, big but too bare and utilitarian: a chair, a desk, a cupboard, a row of filing-cabinets, one solitary picture.

The buzzer told him someone was outside, seeking entry. He depressed a stud and the panel hissed aside and he nearly jumped out of his seat despite the straps.

Gormal swam in. 'I'm Gormal. I thought I ought to say welcome.' A broad lipless mouth moved in what was presumably his head. A resonant voice boomed, 'Welcome.'

'I . . .' the Director fought for composure and found it. 'This is Sciri Pertra. Just Pertra, rather. Glad to know you.'

'Reciprocated.' With Gormal, a smell of filth had entered the office. He noticed Pertra's nostrils wrinkling. 'Sorry. It's from the tank. I like to splash in nice homely muck now and then. Not everyone appreciates the smell.'

'I can believe it,' Pertra said drily. He granted his visitor a long studious look and he saw a creature far from human: immense, roughly ovoid, with a low bulge on top bearing a couple of eyes, a mouth and a flattened nose. A pair of short, blubbery arms stuck out from his shoulders. His legs were even shorter and thicker. Gormal's general appearance was that of something which had been squashed and compressed by unimaginable forces. 'Heavy gravity planet?' the Director asked politely.

'Originally, yes. Very heavy. You'll find it all in my file.' Two huge eyes swung to the cabinets. 'Mammal. Male. Cetaceous. Quite happy in water for long spells. Oxygen-breather. IQ . . . '

'Oh, I'm certain it's nothing to be ashamed of.' Pertra watched in fascination as Gormal hovered like a massive stringless balloon. The buzzer sounded again. Derek dived into the office before the panel had finished opening at Pertra's touch. 'Ah, Mr Derek . . . ' Pertra began.

'Dizzy,' Derek insisted.

'But yes. Yes, exactly – Dizzy. A strange name or nick-name?'

'Aye-aye! Real.' Loose lips wobbled gleefully. 'My parents had a sense of humour. Two senses of humour. Bob and Rhoda, the Chuckling Duo. In a circus.' Pertra laughed sympathetically; Derek giggled pathetically. Through his brain trickled fond memories, mostly fictitious. 'Rhoda fell off a trapeze and had me early. Said she was dizzy from the tumble. So I'm Dizzy because she was. Unique, aren't I?' Compassionately, Pertra nodded. Derek looked gratified. 'Dizzy first name, Derek second. Rhoda Derek. Mother.' He quivered with imbecilic chuckles. 'Father ... '

'Quite!' Pertra realised he had to be firm. The man both amazed and frightened him. A bright brain must lurk some-where in Derek, a glimmer of unusual intelligence clouded by the superficial child-mind. The Director shrugged broad shoulders. Obviously the files would verify Derek's mumblings.

Pertra's eyes lifted, taking in the single decorative feature of his office: a small two-dimensional colour shot of the incredible non-human Tynar, magnetised to a steel disc in the far wall. Beneath it, the Hypothesis was printed in all the languages of the Thirteen. 'Decorative?' wondered Pertra. It struck the eye pleasantly enough, but it hadn't been put there to give aesthetic satisfaction, merely as a reminder of how Theeo had originated and what its purpose was.

The only concessions to ornamentation were the mutable scenes of the Thinkers: Cleo Rosa's arctic snow plains, her flickback to a magic land far distant in space and time. And they weren't wholly for adornment; they had a function. Expediency dictated their presence, not consideration on the part of the Thirteen for the comfort of Theeo's staff.

Pertra thought sadly of the Thirteen. One could hate them without too much effort. Granted, they'd taken a gamble in the first place; Tynar's Hypothesis could have transpired to be no more than the vague theorising of a fool. But not even Tynar's detractors had called him a fool. They'd disagreed with his ideas, dismissed them as being based on hope and sheer speculation rather than solid logic, but they'd never called him a fool. Oh yes, the Thirteen had gambled a little. They'd bet on a possibility so strong it was a probability. That hadn't needed much courage, just faith and luck and money. The Thirteen had found all three and they'd gambled and won. And now they were reaping a rich harvest.

Too rich, in Pertra's opinion.

They held a virtual monopoly on free thought.

Pertra snapped out of his reveries, and remembered that Derek had come in. Plainly he'd come in for a reason. 'Ah Dizzy, my friend, what was it you wanted me for?'

Dizzy blinked. 'I've forgot.'

Chapter Three

Arkon Vitch frequently came on to the surface for the simplest of reasons: to stand and look at the stars. They were rare in Sector 17, but he enjoyed looking at them. They filled him with a wonderful thrill of remoteness, detachment and solitude. At the moment, Silver shared the solitude. Her presence made the thrill no less wonderful. It increased it. He could feel the firmness of her arm locked in his, pleasurable despite the frustration caused by the suit fabric separating them. Behind the mask, her face sparkled argent delight. Her never-kissed lips shaped words into the suit-to-suit radio. 'I could stay out here for ever, Ark.'

'You'd get short of breath after a while.' He started to smile, then the brutal significance of a single word struck him: breath. They shared love, they shared solitude, they shared life, but they couldn't live together properly because they couldn't share breath! He glanced at the lips he could never kiss and remained silent and sullen.

She sensed his mood and the grim thoughts behind it. Speech wouldn't alleviate the gloom. She touched his helmet, eased his head upwards and out. 'Just drink it all in, the vastness of it. Problems dissolve.'

'Maybe.' Grudgingly he recognised truth and let space consume him.

Mostly there was darkness, the deep-black depths of infinity. Here and there tiny motes of brightness burned steadily, somewhere out at the limits of travel and beyond. The faintest suggestion of mistiness, invisible to all but the sharpest of eyes, hinted at the distant Benlhaut Empire: huge, claw-shaped, curled snatchingly around the farthest

24

tip of the Confed. Star 17/LS6 glinted a yellow reminder of the Thirteen.

And there were the Void Regions, of which nothing showed since nothing existed. An enormous sunless hole gaped from the surrounding touches of light on space: a blackness so complete it hurt the mind, an unbelievably absolute absence of light. Like infinity's gigantic hungry mouth, the Void Regions waited gaping.

Wordlessly, Vitch said to himself, 'The Void Regions. Not a sun, not a planet, not a thing. Nothing! Emptiness!' He had the ambition of every Thoughtworlder: to transport Theeo to the place where it could fulfil its purpose to the ultimate – the place of nothingness, of no stargrav, no interference, no impediments. Out there, Thoughtworld could think itself with consummate efficiency through to the mystery of mysteries.

But it was a hopeless ambition, a phantom fantasy.

Silver gazed around Thoughtworld's exterior: a near horizon, a smooth surface scarred by meteors. It was hard to accept that the planetoid had been manufactured, that it wasn't natural; that men and not-men had fabricated a spatial body 10 miles in diameter out of rock, metal and asteroidal debris. It was difficult to believe that everything had been plastimented together and a hollow sphere brought into being with a crust thin enough to conform to stringent weight specifications yet substantial enough to resist meteoric penetration.

Laboriously and ingeniously, the Thirteen had perpetuated Tynar's Hypothesis by creating the solidity to put the theory to trial. And the theory had worked! Thoughtworld was a memorial to Tynar, a hive of high-powered cerebration that hung poised over a dizzying edge, rushing towards a truth which must rock all sentient life to its foundations! But Silver realised that Thoughtworld would function so much more effectively in the Benlhaut Empire or the Void Regions – neither of which it could enter! She swore quietly for a while, looking at metal strips on spools between vertical poles: waiting walkways, to be pinned down when anyone needed to traverse the rock for an appreciable distance in mag-boots. As inside, steel grips covered the outside. Walking on Theeo's surface required a lifeline and plenty of practice: put one foot under a grip, cautiously lift the other, slip it under the next grip a yard farther on. Without detectable gravity, care was vital.

'Makes you feel humble,' Arkon admitted, lowering his gaze from the Benlhaut Empire, the Void Regions, the cosmic deeps. 'We'd be better off in the Empire, Silver.' But he knew Thoughtworld would never get there. Imperial policy seemed to be to obstruct everything the Confed did or suggested, to interpose its colossal might between the Confed and progress.

'No chance.' Non-human, Silver shook her head in a human negative. 'How many times has the Thirteen applied for permission? Fifteen? Twenty? Always the same: no! They don't even bother to be polite.' The Empire's attitude angered her. His Supreme Magnificence Saril onhSaril appeared to despise humans above all other life-forms, but his servants weren't averse to stretching the point to include the whole Confederation – as if merely mixing with humanity contaminated the non-human Confed species and therefore reduced them to a similar despicable status.

The Empire had been offered big money, favourable trade-agreements, the use of Thoughtworld, almost anything, if only the Emperor would allow Theeo to be sited in some near-void area of Imperial space. The benefits to Theeo would be incalculable because parts of Saril onhSaril's dominions were inferior only to the Void Regions.

Yet every offer met with a blunt refusal.

Arm-in-arm, Arkon Vitch and Silver luxuriated in the freedom outside Thoughtworld. Five yards from their feet, an engraved brass plaque embedded in rock marked the grave of eleven men. Somewhere beneath it, eleven corpses lay hidden – unrecovered, mourned briefly and then forgotten. Silver shuddered and thought: 'I might be standing above a body even now!' It had happened in 212, before she was born. In the days when Theeo had been a growing dream, an idea taking form to immortalise Tynar, eleven men had been killed.

Tynar; the Hypothesis; the Conference of Hope, after his death; many difficult problems and bitter arguments; an end to the arguments, a beginning to construction; two years and . . . Thoughtworld! 'Sometimes I can't believe it's real, Ark. Such a fantastic theory, and then to have it proved correct. Why, it's incredible!'

'It's all of that.' He spoke agreeably now, the grey mood had passed. Space really did dissolve problems. Set black enormity against a small black dejection and the dejection had to disappear, swallowed into relative insignificance by the enormity whose true significance nobody could yet fully understand.

He thought: 'We're tiny. We don't count. Just stand and look up . . . '

The ground jumped. It jerked underneath him, slapped one of his feet free of its grip. He clung tight with the other, straining to curl his toes up around it in stiff boots. It wasn't possible, but the foot stayed put. A quick check on his lifeline and he felt more secure, although the ground still jolted and leaped furiously.

Seismic disturbance? Ridiculous! An explosion inside? Possible but unlikely, except there'd been explosions before! Another sabotage attempt? That must be it.

Then he looked over at Silver. Her face-scales were flushed with shock as she screamed, a rising voice scale of terror. Her hands grabbed at nothingness, her feet kicked at nothingness, and she floated through nothingness. Upwards and out. Fast. 'Ark, I'm . . . '

It was a terrible effort to think clearly. Vitch knew that with every passing second she was being drawn towards doom, away from him, out into a space-grave of eternal slowly turning motion. Unless a star sucked her in. Unless a planet caught her. Unless he did something quickly. He deliberately freed his other foot, launching himself rapidly off Thoughtworld. Upwards and out. Fast. It was a risk. If he missed her, he'd lost her forever. He ought to survive, but without her he couldn't be sure that he wanted to.

He prayed he'd judged his course accurately, and could snatch hold of her in the one chance he'd get.

A backward glance showed him a bouncing surface. A forward glance showed him Silver, adrift on an ocean with no end. Her lifeline trailed behind. He noticed the open ring on it, the snap-shut device that, under normal circumstances, anchored it to a grip. The gap between himself and Silver slowly shrank. They still whirled. Some sort of clarity came to Vitch's mind – not the near-total clarity Theeo had been built to induce, only a shadow of it. At least he could concentrate on Silver. His course looked good. Behind him, the lifeline tied him to Thoughtworld like an umbilical cord. It contained his every chance of continued existence. One break would mean two deaths.

He thought frantically: 'Stay shut, snap-shut!' and felt the line paying out from the feed cylinder just above ground-level. He wondered how much rope he had. Silver's fear-filled voice sobbed into his ears, a single name, over and over, 'Ark!' And she uttered pitiful little primal animal sounds, whimpers of ancient horror dredged up through the subconscious from the slough of evolution.

Was he moving quickly enough and in the right direction? He decided he was.

She drifted next to him, within reach. His greater speed wafted him past her and he grabbed an arm just in time. He pulled her to him, clutching her tight. His hand knocked a switch on his suit belt and the lifeline stopped feeding. It locked. Clinging together, they swung like an octopedal pendulum above the inverted clockface of Theeo, hooked on a taut line. Slowly they arced round along the circumference of a circle. 'Arkon . . . thanks!' It sounded inadequate to her, even though her voice expressed all the emotion and gratitude of which she was capable. 'I was scared. I honestly didn't think . . .'

'Don't, then. You're safe.'

'I've learned a lesson. More valuable than everything I learned in school, more priceless than all the fabulous experiences I've had in Thoughtworld. You never really accept how wonderful life is until you see it slipping away. Then you truly appreciate what might have been. What you could and should have done but didn't.'

'I know. You tell yourself, "If ever I get out of this, things are going to be different; I'll make them different." And they stay the same!'

'Cynic,' she said lightly.

'Philosopher.' His quiet chuckle seemed to fill the universe as he put his faceplate next to hers. Suddenly sad, he thought: 'If it's not a helmet, it's a mask. If it's not a mask, it's death!' The grey mood had returned by the time they settled on Theeo.

A foetal position suited Cleo Rosa best. Cosmic immensity frightened her and made her feel like a little girl again, crying into impartial night against forms conjured up by her own imagination. Here near 17/LS6, in the emptiest zone of Confed space, her peculiar agoraphobia hit especially hard. Even inside, she couldn't forget fear of the outside.

She hugged herself to herself, withdrew herself into herself – a tiny ball of beauty, sensual and sylphine. A comfortable scene surrounded her: soft damp walls, cushioning fluid, the circumambient beating of her mother's heart. She wanted to be in a womb, so she was in a womb; in a large brightly lit chamber, yet nevertheless simultaneously in the smallness, darkness and warmth of her mother's womb.

It wasn't by sorcery. It was only a simple helpful consolation. A Thinker needed it, working better with it. Therefore Theeo contained the requisite facilities. Skilfully, Cleo Rosa utilised them to the full.

Beside her in no-grav hung a folder marked 'Urgent'. She had reduced its contents to just one question. With typical endearing audacity, to indicate her distaste of verbosity, she had boldly written on the folder: 'Contents condensed. Would self-government for Karmax be detrimental under the present circumstances?'

Of course it would! Even dim but likeable Derek must realise that. Unhampered, she'd thought the matter through, not that it had needed much mental energy. There was only a single possible answer: the situation on Karmax wouldn't allow self-government. Any fool could see it. Twelve species dwelt on the planet, all xenophobic and hostile, and fighting bitterly among themselves. Often some of them surged offworld to look for trouble elsewhere. Karmax hadn't been out of the top three on the Confed's annual war-incidence list for the past fifty years. It simply couldn't rule itself.

29

Detailing a Thinker to the question had been a waste of time – a query with a built-in answer, doubtless posed by some bureaucrat with nothing better to do. Cleo Rosa cursed for a while in silence, wasting time regretting wasted time.

The non-problematical problem was Confed-initiated, channelled through the Thirteen to Thoughtworld – and at a high price to the Confed, since the Thirteen knew how to charge exorbitantly for services rendered. She felt appalled when she considered how much a few minutes of her mind-work would cost, even on a non-problem!

Dutifully she said into a recorder, 'Autonomy for Karmax could only be disastrous. Recommend Confed continues strict surveillance, severe punishments and direct government from Central.' She paused, then decided to add the impracticable alternative. 'Otherwise forcibly break up Karmax's population and ship it to its original home-worlds.'

This wouldn't work, as they'd soon find their way back again and someday some bureaucrat would set some Thinker the same question. Theeo would return more or less the same answer and so it would go on. She couldn't imagine how the question had got to A-block. Even allowing it to come as far as Thoughtworld had been a mistake. Then unexpectedly she reversed her judgement and conceded that maybe she'd been hasty. Sometimes, so great was the intellectual potential on Theeo, an apparently easy problem could produce a solution no one had ever dreamed of. But this happened rarely. The potential existed, yet mostly it was wasted by bureaucratic fumbling, inefficiency and lack of foresight. Often the Thirteen routed routine stuff to A-block merely to enable the top price to be charged. Cleo Rosa smiled, contemplating what seemed to be the Thirteen's motto: 'Maximum money for minimum endeavour.' Her smile was as cold as a polar waste.

Nearby, thunder bellowed. A loud detonation rattled and echoed through chambers of ringing metal, knocking the womb away, crushing it into oblivion. The beating of her mother's heart changed to the beating of violent and cacophonous shockwaves. Steel walls showed again, walkways, grips and exit panels. Once more, it was a normal room.

Smashed by the blast, Cleo Rosa started spinning. Slowly, still curled up, she rolled through emptiness. The folder, forgotten, curled away. She moved across the room and out of the door, through two more rooms, and she was at the damage area.

Fire glimmered from a jagged-edged hole in the ceiling, and robots were directing foam at the blaze. People stood or hovered, watching: Petra, Dizzy Derek, fat Gormal, others Cleo Rosa didn't recognise. She didn't ask questions. Obviously history had repeated itself. She couldn't see Arkon or Silver anywhere in the press of spectators.

The Director and Gormal looked stunned. As usual Derek looked stupid, but he recovered his presence of mind before the others. To Cleo Rosa's surprise, he grabbed an extinguisher from a pile of spares behind the robots. Then he joined them in the fight against the fire, more mobile, swimming. The robots, magnetically held to the walkways, supplied a steady cannonade of chemicals while Derek took care of the more intricate manoeuvres. He spouted foam and shouted, apparently enjoying himself. The fire died and he flopped down beside the Director, struggling into his boots. 'It's out.'

'Indeed it is. This one is indebted to you, Dizzy.'

'Dizzy? I shouldn't be, when Thoughtworld doesn't spin. But I am, you know. That's really odd.'

The robots filed out with their extinguishers.

'What happened?' Pertra asked.

'Sounded like an explosion,' Gormal said unnecessarily. 'A grenade. A bomb. Not serious, though. Just a minor control for the tinmen.'

Pertra fought desperately against the urge to hold his nose. 'Are similar accidents frequent here?'

'Accidents? Now and then, yes. But this was deliberate.'

'Are you sure?'

'Fairly. Machines don't blow up by spontaneous combustion. Occasionally they fail, but they don't explode. Somebody has to cause them to explode. It was E-block's public lavatory last time. Before that, my tank. Before that ... '

While the Director stared in stupefaction, Gormal listed

ten separate explosions or furtively engineered breakdowns. He went back only two years. Voices backed him up, agreed with every detail pulled from his phenomenal memory.

'So some agency seeks to destroy Theeo?'

'Not at all. Only slight damage and inconvenience. Annoyance tactics.' Gormal paused, his voice altering to a dramatic roar when he continued. 'Plus an attempt to hijack us by long-range tractor beam. Luckily, Squadron 17 were in the area and they snapped it by some military magic.'

'Oh,' Pertra said weakly. He'd heard of the Confed's regular checks to see Theeo was safe. One aspect of the affair amused him: the Thirteen hadn't sufficient weapons to do the job themselves, so to their disgust they were forced to hire Squadron 17. For this, the Confed charged over the odds.

'Benlhaut,' Gormal pronounced ominously. 'That's who. Though why they indulge in petty sabotage as well, I couldn't say. Perhaps to scare us off so they can pinch Thoughtworld empty.'

At the mention of Benlhaut, Pertra's grey face turned greyer.

The robots trooped back in to clean up. Five of them, wearing mag-boots, walked up the walls and along the ceiling. As far as the walkways permitted, they leaned to the jagged-edged hole and sliced off the tangled steel with heat torches. One robot held an extensible trellis device terminating in a large magnet. It passed its time catching chunks of metal, bringing them to hand with the gadget and attaching them to a magnetised band running down each leg. Some of the torch-bearers used grips when possible, then clunked back feet-first to the walkways. A highly specialised welding robot was also employed. It progressed booted as far as it could and stopped by the hole. To do its job, it needed both hands; the grips were out. Also it had to be under the hole and able to move freely; the walkways were out. Nor were robots very clever in no-grav. So, from a box on its back it extruded six slim rods, each tipped with a swivel-fitted sucker pad. The rods elongated, finally stuck to floor, ceiling and all four walls. Slowly the robot adjusted them – a yard along a wall here, two yards along the floor there – until it rested like some grotesque insect right beneath the hole. Then it began to weld on a steel disc which had been brought up in the meantime. Buzzes issued from beyond the disc: robot repairmen fixing the damaged mechanism, skilled non-life.

Stealth would have been useless. Worse, it would have invited suspicion. Lights blazed everywhere and Thinkers of all grades wafted through no-grav on various errands: low-levellers bringing complex problems to A-block, students hopefully searching for a top-flight Thinker with a moment to spare. A few people moved about less speedily on the walkways. Robots clicked and whirred past, always busy. One figure lost itself among many and made no effort to stay hidden. It wasn't possible, and a furtive demeanour would have aroused unwanted glances.

The figure drifted down a corridor, not too quickly, not too slowly. It carried camouflage which couldn't have been recognised as camouflage: an armful of folders. Outside Communications it stopped. Naturally, it went into the empty room. Strangely, precautions were more necessary here out of sight than outside in open view. A brisk motion locked the door – abnormal behaviour, but several words would explain it: 'Sorry. I must have brushed the button with my elbow. Come on in.'

The visiplate warmed up instantly at the flick of a switch. Fingers journeyed over the keys to punch a many-digited number. Hands grew damp. Time stretched. There'd be checks, hasty intercom calls, re-routing through a couple of exchanges – not so much delay as usual on this line, but still patience was needed. The plate remained blank. No one came to the door.

Lundren appeared on the screen. 'Successful?'

'So-so. Quite effective.'

'Where did you put it?'

'In an ancillary robot control unit, to cripple some of them. At the heart, in A-block. I'd say roughly under the plaque.'

Colour drained from Lundren's face. 'Under the plaque?'

Gradually the pallor surrendered to a flush of anger. 'You fool! You're supposed to be able to think up there! You . . . ' He stopped when the communicant stared at him in astonishment. 'Forget it!'

A mistake, thought Lundren moodily. I made a mistake there. Showed a card that only I should know about. That dupe couldn't realise how close we came there. Too damned close to feel easy!

'I don't understand.'

'Don't try!' snapped Lundren, thinking: 'I just revealed the reverse side of the card, fortunately! Nevertheless, no one else should know it even exists!' Too proud and stubborn to admit his error, he dismissed it and went on more quietly. 'Did they connect it with earlier strikes?'

'Obviously. And erroneously, in part. The tractor beam last year . . . '

'Benlhaut, definitely!' Certitude made Lundren's voice ring loudly, but he disguised his uncertainty about why Saril onhSaril should try to drag off Theeo. Surely he didn't expect to get away with theft so blatant as that? Or perhaps he did. Thought followed such different paths out in the Empire. 'And the others?'

'All attributed to the same party.'

'Good.' A mirthless smile touched the old face. 'I'll carry on knocking pieces off what I built. We'll simply have to hope the Emperor has no better fortune in any future stunts he's planning.' Briefly, Lundren wondered exactly what Saril onhSaril's reasons were. 'Let the fuss die down, then hit them again. That's all.'

'No, it isn't!'

Lundren froze in the act of reaching out to break contact, and scowled at the contradiction. 'I beg your pardon?' he asked, far too quietly.

'I said there's more.'

'Such as?'

'Such as Dizzy Derek. He's worried me for a while; I've been watching him. He's cracked, true! But do you know who he is?'

Impatience darkened Lundren's features. 'A fool who must possess sufficient ability to be useful to the Thirteen, although he hides it well, I hear. Tell me, then: who is he?'

The communicant told him.

'A complication,' Joab Lundren confessed. 'How did you find out?'

'I sneaked a look at his file.'

'I see. It could be coincidence. It could mean nothing. However . . . ' A frown came through the visiplate. 'It could mean trouble. I'm a great believer in playing safe. Get rid of him!'

Chapter Four

Lundren swept aside a dozen papers to produce a clear space on his desk. Smugly he set down a book entitled *The Ones Who Made Today*. From abundant usage, it fell open at the right page and he read a short but significant section: 'JOAB LUNDREN: Born in 177 on Morlin (Phorac II), the son of an army captain. At the age of nineteen, Lundren collaborated with the celebrated Tynar on the latter's revolutionary Hypothesis which was directly responsible for the building of Theeo. In 209, when representatives of the thirteen planets with faith in the Hypothesis met at the Conference of Hope to discuss the possible creation of Theeo, it is said by many persons present that Lundren almost single-handed pushed the project through. It is hardly ever disputed that his drive and determination ultimately swung the balance in favour of constructing a world to test the Hypothesis. A paradoxical man, the peace-loving Lundren, who played such a large part in the colonisation of New Athens in 197, later entered the harsh world of politics, admittedly less vicious on New Athens than anywhere else in the charted universe. Educated at the Morlin Academy, he graduated with honours in the Social Sciences in 193, at sixteen the youngest scholar ever to do so in the Academy's history. He is now Prime Minister of New Athens and one of Thoughtworld's most vociferous admirers.'

Lundren snapped the book shut, then placed it in a drawer. He handled it carefully after the initial angry closing, almost religiously, as if it were a sacred relic. In a way it was, for it summarised his life and his life was to him a sacred treasure, not life in general but Joab Lundren's life in particular, simply because it was Joab Lundren's. He believed in himself more than in any deity. He read the message every day without fail to remind himself who he was, what he was and how he'd got there. It always thrilled him to go over his career again: the finalising of the Hypothesis with Tynar, the mass emigration that ended on New Athens, the exciting though arduous task of thrashing down all opposition and swinging the Conference of Hope towards an affirmative backed by hard cash.

Yet every good memory bore a concomitant bad one.

He couldn't forgive Tynar for accepting all the praise for the Hypothesis; Lundren had done his share of the research, but Tynar had never publicly acknowledged it. He'd just drunk in the eulogies. And what about the settling of New Athens? A labour of love, true, yet a hard one! Eleven species to handle, to disperse over the world at the foundation of Peace Planet. Then the battle with the Confed, to convince the authorities that they should waive their right to a levy from New Athens for the Confederation Armed Forces.

Fighters from Peace Planet? Unthinkable!

Thus he'd argued. He'd promised tranquillity on his world, no army, no need of one. He'd pledged himself to internal harmony in return for exemption. After thirty years of placidity, rebellion had burst out, grown, festered, and culminated in Lev Merrin, only to increase again after the insurgence had been put down. This made the Enforcement Agency necessary, secret killers paid in secret. He was constantly afraid that the Confed would learn of the EA, and that Peace Planet's good name would be wrecked, perhaps his own reputation would be besmirched, possibly a Confed military base would be established on New Athens, and autonomy would be lost. The idea obsessed him, haunted sleep.

Sadly he gazed at a framed script on a wall, the words of a long-dead poet whose name no one remembered:

Another Athens shall arise,
And to remoter time
Bequeath, like sunset to the skies,
The splendour of its prime;

And leave, if nought so bright may live,
All earth can take or Heaven can give.

Well, the verse just wasn't applicable any more. *This* Athens
had passed the splendour of its prime and entered its Dark
Age. Rebellion in 238, muted mutterings still, the strong
silent EA – a dreadful story, Lundren reflected.

'The drastic measures I've had to adopt to keep the secret,'
he said quietly to himself: the supposed "screening" of
people as they came to New Athens. It had been straightforward screening at first, but today it was much worse.

His thoughts switched to Theeo. What devious game
was the Benlhaut Empire playing? Could he outmanoeuvre
the Emperor? Did Saril onhSaril intend to abduct Theeo,
or were his schemes deeper and more subtle than mere
theft? What was Dizzy Derek doing up there? Coincidence?
Could be. Or did the man have plans? He might have. Either
way, he had to be eliminated. Lundren was glad he'd given
the order.

The date-panel read 7–4–245. 'Day 8 tomorrow,' Derek
estimated accurately, looking forward to it. Every year, Day
8 of Fourmonth witnessed a change of routine in Thoughtworld. 'It appeals to my morbid streak,' Derek mumbled.

No one paid any attention to him. He was such an extra-
ordinary character that his colleagues now considered him
nothing out of the ordinary – a figure floating rapidly through
A-block, talking to himself and replying amicably. He was
commonplace.

Flecks of saliva dripped from his slack mouth. 'Sorry,
robots! You don't mind, do you? No, of course you don't.
How can you mind when you haven't any minds?' Then
he said, 'Another pun,' and shrieked with laughter.

Nobody bothered.

Derek nodded now and then to people he either knew or
didn't. Brilliant light flooded the corridors as he made his
way back to his quarters after a tiring session in Think. He
was ready for bed, with or without supper, depending on
whether or not he remembered to eat. The lights went out.

A slight suggestion of vibration was in the air, an electronic call to the robots closest to whichever mechanism had malfunctioned. Derek felt it plainly, although not everyone's senses were as acute as his. The robots would soon repair the lights. They were very quick. Say five or six minutes and ...

He was being strangled. A thin cutting cord noosed his throat, tightening. He heard the heavy breathing of exertion near him in the total darkness. He didn't want to be strangled. In nothing, he kicked out and met clothing. Then he punched hard and fast, left–right–left, and his fists hit air. The cord tautened further on his neck as the assailant twisted in no-grav to avoid unseen but expected blows. He or she – or even it, since there were several neuters in Theeo – seemed to be angling round towards Derek's back, out of reach. Yes, the grunts came from behind him now. Hands pulled at the cord. He couldn't breathe!

His hands tore at the constricting rope and he managed to slip a fingertip under it. The next breath, little better than a gulping gasp, was the sweetest he'd ever drawn. He tried to slide the finger further under, but it wouldn't go. In fact it was slowly being squeezed out by the cord. His nostrils gaped open, narrowed, sniffing in tiny drags of air. But hardly any of it got through to his lungs. He writhed, twitched, kicked, scratched – at nothing. Then, relying on all his skill in weightlessness, he swung his legs up high in front of him, then slammed his feet back in a powerful curving heel-kick.

He struck flesh. Somebody groaned in pain and he took advantage of a momentary slackening of the cord. Both hands flew up and he snatched it, tugging forward and launching himself away as forcibly as he could. If he were lucky, he should get free. If his opponent hung on tightly enough, he might break his neck. His neck stayed intact, and Derek found himself still diving forward in the dark. Occasionally he blundered into someone and heard angry comments about people sky-diving during a light failure. He ignored them and finally bumped solidly against a wall. It hurt his head, but he could tolerate the kind of agony that didn't choke off his breath. He almost enjoyed it. He remained exactly where he was – crumpled up at some indefinable point on a wall – and waited. The cord had fallen off somewhere. Eventually the lights flashed on and he studied the view: walkers standing frozen on walkways, a fair number of Thinkers gently floating, all innocence.

After peeling himself off the wall, he made it with a thundering heart back to the safety of his rooms. The first place he headed for was the lavatory. 'These horrible suction toilets!' he thought uncomfortably. 'I'll never be happy with them!' They felt as if they were pulling his insides out. To a certain extent, they were.

Derek woke from a nightmare, sweat-wet and trembling. He couldn't recollect details, just a frightful miscellany of rattling explosions, buffeting bodies, expressionless robots, and the memory of strangulation. Derek asked himself questions. They were glimmerings in a murky night, sluggish thoughts in a murky brain. Who had tried to kill him? And why? There was nothing special about him. Then a searing bolt of contradiction rocked his mind: 'Yes, there is, there is! Much that's special! Someday . . .'

The mental chain snapped and another one took over. Was there any connection between the attack on him and the attacks on Thoughtworld? No, there couldn't be. They must be separate incidents stemming from separate motives. He wished he understood either motive. Because there couldn't be any connection, could there? Unless somebody intended to annihilate Thoughtworld simply in order to annihilate Derek! In which case, why set a killer inside Thoughtworld and endanger the hired assassin's life too? Or didn't the power behind the assault care about his underlings? Was the assailant merely a form of insurance to ensure Derek's death in case the attempts to destroy Thoughtworld failed?

'Doesn't add up,' Derek muttered, tired yet incapable of sleep. 'They can't be after Thoughtworld merely to get me. Because why get me? I've not done anybody any harm. Yet.' He giggled. 'Yet!' And then he saw the flaw in his reasoning: nobody had ever tried to destroy Thoughtworld. Admittedly, they had tried to capture it, but these attempts were neither really serious nor dangerous – just isolated damage from time to time, not a single injury apart from scratches and bruises. Theeo had suffered one attempted theft, foiled by Squadron 17, and a host of scattered inconveniences.

Derek squirmed restlessly in the cocoon, a fine-stranded web used by those who preferred not to sleep strapped down to a normal bed. Four rods stuck from the nominal ceiling, two at the head, two at the feet. Between them was suspended the silky net envelope into which the occupant wriggled.

The cocoons allowed plenty of movement. They were comfortable, secure, ideal for rest or sleep – but with one glaring disadvantage which suddenly occurred to Derek: you couldn't get out quickly if somebody came in to kill you!

Then Derek took up a new line of reasoning.

Why shouldn't there be two agencies responsible for the trouble in Theeo? He couldn't think of a reason why there should be *one*, but nevertheless, why shouldn't there be two? Derek settled for two different parties, but he was at a loss to imagine what each expected to gain. Like most things, it baffled him. The alternative to two enemies seemed to be an alien autocrat whose brain could see a valid purpose in firstly making the effort to race off with Thoughtworld, then later – and also beforehand, come to that – crippling relatively unimportant parts of it.

The door buzzed.

Derek tensed. 'Who is it?'

In tones of thunder, a voice said, 'Gormal'.

Must be Gormal, Derek decided. You can't fake a voice like his. And who'd want to? I'm nervous and feeling persecuted. Next, I'll be fancying someone's trying to kill me. 'Someone is!' he yelled, remembering.

'I beg your pardon?'

'I said come in.' He was far enough out of the cocoon now to make an airborne break for it, if necessary. It wouldn't be easy to catch him in no-grav. He knew he was good. 'Come in.'

'I can't. The wretched door's locked.'

'That's right, I remember locking it. Just a minute.' Derek

41

floated to the button, pressed it, and leapt back warily. He was ensconsed in the furthest top corner when Gormal walked in, in boots.

The cetacean turned to the cocoon, goggling at its emptiness. 'Where are you?' Bulbous eyes rolled a gaze upwards. 'Oh, there you are! What's the idea?' He stared through gloom at a cornered shape.

'Exercises.' Derek left it at that and asked, more sharply than he'd meant to, 'What do you want?'

'Called in to chat. I was just passing and it's obvious you weren't asleep. You were talking to yourself.'

'Was I? I didn't realise.'

'You seldom do.' Uninvited, Gormal flicked on the light. 'That's better. Excuse my smell, but what shall we chat about?'

'Anything.' Derek was playing for time. His head had suddenly filled with unpleasant thoughts. What if there were only one enemy, after all? That would mean whoever was trying to steal Theeo was trying to sabotage it piecemeal also. Derek hadn't been able to make up his mind which of the two had attacked him, if either, and reducing the enemy to one almost certainly meant that the saboteur/thief had Derek's assassination on his list. Or did a third party exist?

He worked backwards along a somewhat confusing string of incidents.

Attack on me – minor sabotage – attempt to steal Theeo.

Vaguely, he reasoned that the person responsible for incident three was behind incident one and incident two. And the person responsible for incident three was Emperor Saril onhSaril. Therefore Saril onhSaril had plans to effect a successful incident one, Derek's murder.

The Emperor hated humans and would in all probability employ a non-human killer/saboteur. Which narrowed the possibilities: Silver definitely alien; Sciri Pertra, a human-looking although perhaps not fully human being, plus approximately 300 other aliens in Thoughtworld. Plus Gormal, who was in his room at that moment! Derek trembled in his corner, frightened. His stomach felt queer again. Still, he had the advantage if the worst came to the worst.

Gormal wore boots; Derek didn't. Even in no-grav, Gormal wouldn't stand much chance of catching him. Except he stood between Derek and the door! If he started to unbuckle his boots . . .

'Nice day,' Gormal said conversationally, realising Derek might remain dumb forever. 'They're all the same, of course, but . . . '

Derek stayed mute, thinking hard. It couldn't be Gormal. He wouldn't have needed a strangling cord. There was strength enough in those massive arms to throttle anyone bare-handed, with no chance of breaking away. Also, he could easily snap the spine of any creature in Thoughtworld. So it isn't Gormal, Derek mused. But even so, I'm not too thrilled by the fact that he's here. For a chat? Okay. Although I feel vulnerable. 'Yes.' Emboldened by the steadiness of his voice, he pursued the conversation. 'Yes.'

'Yes what? Oh, I see. A nice day. Yes.' Gormal decided the man couldn't talk sense.

Dizzy, still thoroughly on edge and nervous, glanced at a cupboard. He felt scared for what was locked in it: his most treasured possession, retained to keep his hate burning – a small book, neatly handwritten, but now the writer was dead. She'd been a beautiful girl, once. He'd never seen her alive, yet he knew she'd been beautiful, before it happened. No, he couldn't bear the memory. But he couldn't ward it off either. Her red lips, which would never kiss again. Her ripe young body, her corn-gold hair. And those hideous bulging blue dead eyes!

'Gormal, there's no mercy outside Heaven. They talk of Hell, Gormal. I think Hell's being alive. For some people, death isn't the gate to Heaven; it *is* Heaven.'

Gormal found himself speechless in the face of Derek's unusual fervour and coherence. Something must be riding him devilishly hard!

Fastened to a walkway, Arkon Vitch pondered what environment to Think in. How about a pleasant scene of home, the blue hills and redstone quarries of Phorac III? No, Phorac III wasn't home any longer; Thoughtworld was.

Why resurrect painful memories of a harsh infancy and youth? Not Phorac III, then. Perhaps he'd surround himself with women, unreal models posing as real flesh. He decided against it, as it would be a form of intellectually two-timing Silver. She didn't deserve that. He'd create the home for which he yearned, the home in which he could never live: Silver's world.

Unbuckled, the boots clung to metal as Arkon took off. He levelled out in the middle of the room, stopped himself and lay horizontal. The folder – doubtless not so urgent as it pretended – he hung on air beside him. Then he Thought his environment.

Distant ice mountains rimmed a horizon no farther away than the walls of the room. Pale lightning slashed an infinite grey sky as near as the ceiling. He rested warm in a bed of cold snow, a dozen yards above the floor. He was on Silver's world.

Inside Theeo.

Sometimes the spot itched. Sometimes you could actually feel the microscopic device surgically implanted under the skull. Occasionally you heard – or only imagined you heard? – it relay its impulses, your premeditated desires, to much larger electronic miracles all around the Think chamber: machines which translated patterns of thought into patterns of colour, intangible but visible images, engineered dreams. Outside the head, inside Theeo. The environments were conducive to relaxation. Relaxation was conducive to lucid thought. Thoughtworld had been designed to produce lucid thought, so the Thirteen had provided the means of relaxation. Also no-grav, as dictated by Tynar's Hypothesis.

Vitch made several adjustments to depth, colour, perspective. Images melted, then came into being exactly as he wanted them. He was on Silver's world. The room *was* Silver's world, both to its creator and to a spectator. It would stay that way until he chose to obliterate the colours, or until some unexpected external stimulus jarred it out of his mind and out of existence. He could hold it for the rest of his life, mentally compartmentalised yet always there, requiring no more thought than did breathing. If he forgot to unthink it, the chamber would retain it until he eventually

44

remembered; an empty room of unattractive steel, with a whole view of Silver's world within its bleak confines. Often, Thinkers deliberately didn't unthink their scenes. They left them behind as decorations after a session in Think.

Arkon Vitch organised his thoughts prior to tackling the folder. Next door, Gormal sung merrily but tunelessly of home, with all the noise of a friendly storm:

'Cloud-ships sailing seas of sky, sun-ship
    sinking over world-lip,
'Sinking into womb of Ocean;
'Roaring wind and painted mountain, rock-tip
    painted on the . . .'

Vitch switched Gormal completely out of his mind. He looked at the folder, checked his recorder and thought. Slowly and purposefully he worked his way through a series of unrelated ideas. Not everybody did it like this, but Vitch preferred to lead up to Think gradually, climb over other things with no relevance to the folder. He saw Think as one of Gormal's mountains. First you ascend a foothill idea, then clamber up a low cliff, then scale a precipice, little by little overcoming the think rocks until you reach the flat summit of Think.

So he thought of the annual ceremony in a couple of hours: he hated it. Each year it upset Silver more. She was very sensitive. The reminder of death plunged her into gloom all day. Day? Day 8, Fourmonth, 212. Thirty-three years ago. It disturbed him because it disturbed her. Exactly as it disturbed him to think of methane, ammonia, masks. Lips he couldn't kiss. Although there were other beautiful lips he could kiss if he wished, the lips of Cleo Rosa: Black Rose. A rare beauty. But he didn't love her. Silver was the ultimate desire of his life, the penultimate step of his ascent. He paused, tasting her name: Silver. Then forgot her and climbed up on to the clear-sky summit of Think.

Chapter Five

Words droned monotonously in Silver's ears: 'Let space which bends above us shield their bones. Let the stars be God's eyes and watch over them. Let them lose all taint of Sin in the physical dissolution accompanying assimilation with the All. We pray for their souls as we mourn their bodies. Far from home they came, and far from home they died. We beseech the God Who manifests Himself as every god in the Universe . . . '

She wanted to scream at the banality of it, yell at somebody to stop the voice. But it was a recording, tinny and maddening. The only switch that would kill it rested on Sciri Pertra's belt, under his thumb. He looked uncomfortable and bored, as if he'd like nothing better than to squash the words. His thumb twitched now and then. Silver glanced away from his restless thumb, and looked upwards to the Void Regions, black-on-black, a fruitless ambition, and to the Benlhaut Empire, a faint sight but a glaring threat, a mystery, the realms of an incomprehensible sovereign. She looked anywhere except at the mass grave, bizarre in the ghost-glow of temporary lighting.

Arkon squeezed her arm. 'Don't worry.' She couldn't help it. 'Death in Thoughtworld,' she thought. 'Eleven corpses somewhere beneath our feet.' Granted it had only been an accident. Nothing brutal, nothing vicious. Simply a tragic cave-in, caused by ill-luck or perhaps negligence, made possible by the colossal grav-generators the contractors had been using at the time. Eleven men buried, swallowed up in the crust of a planetoid they were helping to build. Eleven humans killed, a curious fact, since many a race had been engaged on the work. Still, only a coincidence. Only an

46

accident. But nevertheless, there was death on Thought-world even before its completion. *'An omen!'* shrieked a deep part of her mind. *'A bad one!'*

The tinny voice droned on.

Theeo's personnel formed a circle centred on the plaque. Some were uneasy, some relaxed, some enjoying it, some not. Silver wondered why they'd come, and why she'd come. She felt a sense of duty, a feeling that she was showing respect for the dead she'd never known. She hated it, but she came. How many others among the gathered hundreds did the same?

Every Day 8, Fourmonth, the deceased were remembered, and played into each helmet were words relating to physical dissolution, a state which the preacher who prattled these sentiments might himself be undergoing. Assimilation with the All? Had even he believed it? Did anyone here today believe it? Certainly Silver didn't.

Thoughtworld wasn't the place for memorial services, religion, and metaphysical speculation. It dealt with facts, science, and knowledge, not theory. Yet it had been founded on a theory.

'And,' persisted Silver's inner voice, against her will, 'you've overlooked something. You've overlooked . . . '

'The Breakthrough . . . '

'Isn't that religion? At least, isn't it – or won't it soon be – an answer? And what is religion but answers? Right or wrong, it doesn't matter! Religions are the answers to questions the brain isn't capable of even framing properly. Answers accepted without proof, without need of proof. Religions hang on faith, not demonstrable evidence!'

'With the Breakthrough, there'll be evidence!' But the problem would be in demonstrating it.

' . . . in God's Holy Name,' rattled the recording, 'we entreat Eternity to smile upon their eleven souls. Let this world, this creation within Creation – Tynar's Hypothesis Experimental Environment One – be both their tomb and their epitaph. Amen.'

'Ah-bloody-men!' sighed Derek, although he'd enjoyed it. He himself couldn't understand his relief at the cessation of enjoyment. 'That appealed to my morbid streak.' He knew everyone on-surface could hear him, but it didn't matter.

Affable enquiries were directed at him: 'You okay, Derek?' 'Ready for dinner, Dizzy?' He answered them all by nodding, thinking: 'That's no answer at all, but it'll do.' They always asked silly questions, nearly always called him Dizzy. *They must think I'm stupid, which I am. Must believe that stuff about my name.* Occasionally he believed it himself; occasionally he forgot the truth. The small book helped:

> 'The life still there upon her hair –
> 'The death upon her eyes.'

Nearby, Cleo Rosa felt dampness on her dark cheeks, and tasted salt as it touched her lips. She'd never even read the names of the eleven men. They'd lived and died a decade before her birth, but she could cry for them and shed tears for dead strangers. She concluded that she was too emotional. Too much the woman, too little the Thinker. 'Gormal, I . . .' Words failed her and she rested a slim gloved hand on his immense arm; not with affection, merely for companionship, and yet not without affection, she realised. He was non-human, huge and ugly, but at the moment his size was a bulwark against the ambient emptiness, a vacancy so inconceivable it pressed down like the weight of a thousand worlds.

He let her hand lie there, spoke solely to her through a hundred other conversations which had sprung up as soon as Dizzy had shattered what might have become a reverent silence. He was conscious of the din, but his voice, unusually subdued, picked out only Cleo Rosa, caressed her with its quiet proximity verging on intimacy. 'You weep, Dark Flower?'

'I weep, Gormal. For men whose names I don't know. Am I foolish?'

'Not foolish; different, that's all. Different emotionally. To me, for instance.'

'Can't you cry, Gormal? Don't you have emotions?'

'Yes and scores of them, respectively. Different emotions, though. Happy-joy at a new birth. Sad-joy when the sun

48

dies each evening, drowned in Ocean. Happy-joy when it's born again. *Bhrilla* when I ride a fast wave. *An'laBhrilla* under a crush of water, coasting deep. But none that allow of crying for the dead who won't be reborn. For the dead who, unlike the sun . . '

'I think I understand, Gormal,' she said quietly.

'I believe you do, Bloom of Night. Truly I believe it!' And with surprising tenderness, his hand fell leaf-light upon hers, an interspecies contact transcending words. Still the other conversations clamoured as the crowd began to break up, but between Gormal and Cleo Rosa lay a silence of mutual respect which could only have suffered by the violation of words. No words broke their silence, but Cleo Rosa's thoughts shattered the spell. She couldn't shake off an imagination-picture of partially completed Theeo thirty-three years ago: an enormous hole, with eleven men somewhere in it, dead or dying. There must have been a rescue operation, a failure. Then the difficult decision to call a halt, to give the men up for lost. Then a brief funeral service, the words she'd just heard taped, listened to in silence in the middle of nowhere by representatives of every party with an interest in Theeo: Erranlal on behalf of his brother Tynar, President Darren for Hope, Joab Lundren for New Athens, other people from the Thirteen. Then machines shovelling the hole full again, entombing eleven corpses.

The attack came. It came as a sudden quiet. Conversations died as though at a prearranged signal, but no signal had been given. Nobody had looked up yet. Nobody knew. Yet conversations died spontaneously, without the erstwhile talkers realising why they'd died. Somebody looked up. Everybody looked up.

And there they were, drifting down from space like lethal pollen: a task-force of fifty or sixty, their backs breathing the flames of blast-packs. Seven ships waited high and motionless. They could have been steel clouds, sprinkling living raindrops over Theeo.

'Invasion!' thought Gormal, tensing. 'They've chosen a bad time, with so many of us up top!' Then he realised they hadn't chosen badly at all. They'd chosen remarkably well. 'We're herded together, just waiting to be surrounded. Or picked off by the dozen!' Or would they do it less messily? Simply cut the lifelines, kick feet clear of grips, and then the long float off into death and nowhere would begin. Voices broke out again agitatedly, but Gormal kept calm. He watched, patiently searching for a weakness. Numerically, the attackers were inferior. Surprisingly, only about a tenth of them had weapons. Still, a tenth was more than enough. Didn't they have any weaknesses, then?

'Yes, they did!' Gormal chuckled, expecting a laugh before long. Not that the situation was exactly funny, but it promised to show an amazing side shortly – if he'd assessed things correctly. He ignored the voices, even Cleo Rosa's, and studied the invaders as they approached. He counted nine different species, some appeared human although likely they were non-humans who were constructed similarly. You couldn't really tell with a suited figure. Saril onhSaril wouldn't use the humans he despised so much. Or would he? You couldn't really tell with the Emperor, either.

The nearest attackers were almost down, scattering wide over Theeo. 'Now for the fun,' thought Gormal. He was willing to wager a year's salary against the Emperor's troops having come properly prepared. On Thoughtworld, walking conditions tended to be slightly disconcerting unless you'd practised a lot. The creatures all seemed to be wearing standard-issue mag-boots, but boots wouldn't help because the surface walkways were spooled, not laid out. Even without weapons, the advantage must be with the Thoughtworlders. 'If we could only bring them closer somehow,' thought Gormal.

The first invader touched down, blast-pack switched off. It seemed to bounce, then tried once more to land. It scrambled for a grip, missed, and started to float away up the sky-path down which it had arrived. Its comrades were experiencing the same trouble. A few caught grips, but not many. They stood uncertain, while reinforcements arrived to try and help them.

'Never underestimate gravity,' muttered Gormal. 'Especially when it isn't there.' A fat smile crossed his contorted face. Saril onhSaril's minions weren't going to have much luck unless they learned about the spooled walkways. His.

train of thought was interrupted as he caught sight of Derek hurrying to a spool. He reached it and began to pull out the metal strip. Gormal grimaced. Admittedly it was stalemate at the moment – the assailants could not do a great deal of harm to Theeo since they were unable to stick to its surface in sufficient numbers – but it wouldn't take a great deal to upset the balance. It would only take a single traitor to pull out several strips. It would only take Dizzy Derek . . .

'Gormal!' A cry lashed through the stupefied silence. It was Derek's voice, abnormally loud and urgent. 'Gormal! Spools! Unwind, rewind!'

At first it didn't make sense. Then suddenly it did, and Gormal felt honoured to have been selected. 'Okay, Dizzy, I get it.'

Hoping that the rest of the Thoughtworlders would remain numbed by shock and not try to stop him, Gormal deliberately threw off his lifeline. It was an encumbrance. He'd have to rely on his ability to grip-walk. If anyone did try to halt him, he knew he'd need to get tough, for Thoughtworld's sake. He considered it unlikely anyone would come at him, but the weaker Derek was a different matter. Understandably, they might gang up on him and prevent him finishing what he'd started. They might conceivably even gang up on Gormal himself, but he could only pray they wouldn't.

They decided to take Derek first.

A group of youngsters had snapped out of astonishment. Lifelines discarded, they set off towards Derek. A quiet but authoritative voice froze them: 'Remain where you are, please!' But Pertra wasn't asking; he was telling! And the group took no notice. 'I repeat: remain where you are!' The Director's tone was still level and steady. 'Otherwise Thoughtworld will be rid of you within the month. Forever. That is a solemn promise, not a threat.' They hesitated just long enough to perceive a glimmer of what was really happening. Obediently, they stopped. The minority who'd also seen the light gazed at Dizzy with respect. But the majority were still in the figurative dark, under the ultimate unchanging dark. They spoke of treachery in scared voices. Shrill expletives from Cleo Rosa burned like acid in Gormal's brain.

Fourteen of the outsiders had succeeded in sticking to the surface. Statuesque, they seemed content just to cling to grips. Not one shot had been fired. 'This is comedy,' thought Gormal. 'It shouldn't be, but it is. It should be deadly serious!' But an upward glance told him it *was* deadly serious. The Imperial troops hadn't come to kill. They'd come to steal.

From one of the ships, a score of huge devices dropped slowly, guided by remote-controlled blasts. Suddenly frightened, Gormal recognised them: grapplers. When the advance party had established a foothold on Theeo, the grapplers would be strategically placed by them. Each one would bore inexorably through the crust, sealing as it went. Inside, they'd blossom into gigantic, powerful, inverted umbrella-frames. And nothing would budge them until somebody up aloft pressed the right buttons and the blossoms closed again and withdrew.

Gormal shuddered. The operation was crude and clumsy, not so sophisticated as a tractor beam, but definitely effective and definitely capable of stealing Theeo. Yet how did the Emperor expect to sneak off across the length of the Confed with Thoughtworld in tow, undetected? Maybe the Emperor didn't operate by the rules of common sense. Maybe he didn't believe in it. Maybe sense wasn't common out here. Maybe practically anything, mused Gormal, confused.

Suddenly Gormal came out of his reverie and realised the need for action. He quickly moved towards spools, trying not to hear Cleo Rosa. Derek already had a strip laid out, deliberately pinned down only by an absolute minimum of pins. He made gestures, telling the attackers by sign language to set down on the walkway. Aimed by blast-pack bursts, they did. Packs flared. Boots clicked and clung. Stranded colleagues gleefully yielded themselves to space, then returned to safer ground with sporadic boot clunks. Derek laid his second strip at right-angles to the first and formed a large L enclosing two sides of the crowd. At his signal, bodies flitted over to occupy it. Humming tunelessly, he stood by the two spools he'd used. He was equidistant from each, waiting.

Gormal copied Dizzy's actions. He made another L on

the other two sides and thought: 'L + L = a square, if they're arranged properly.' Which they were. His L, added to Derek's L, made a square containing the throng around the plaque. The throng murmured dangerously about foul sedition. Several individuals seemed on the verge of interfering, but Pertra's promise was keeping them irresolute. All four strips now held occupiers. All the attackers were down, securely magnetised. If they were amazed at the unexpected help, they didn't show it. They simply took advantage of it and watched the twenty grapplers closing in.

Gormal, too, stool equidistant from his pair of spools. 'We've got them concentrated. Not spread out. Now wait. Wait for the word,' he told himself. He steadied his legs, readied his arms and prepared to act. The word came 'Now!' As he shouted, Derek pounced. Gormal pounced also. Cautiously yet swiftly, grip-tripping, they leapt to their spools. Hands blurred, slapping switches, and highly tensile springs inside the spools did their silent implacable duty. They whipped their strips in, fast. Pins tore loose, slashed up sharp. Three suits were punctured – three less to worry about. Creatures floundered as the ground did a speedy slither from under them, like a slimy serpent bouncing fleas off its back. Outsiders, flapped up into space, did their best to flap down again using blast-packs. They touched land, only to see it recede rapidly because it hadn't the gravity to retain them. Bodies flew up, blasted down, grabbed at grips and missed, and the pattern was repeated again and again.

Dizzy Derek had turned fear into farce, robbery into rout. 'Move, please!' urged Pertra, still quiet-voiced. 'We have a task.' As an example, he cast off his lifeline. He was far from confident, but he did it. Most of the others did the same. Hundreds of lines would have resulted in an impossible tangle, an unnecessary complication. Pertra led the way with careful-stepping determination. His untrained army followed and the Battle of Thoughtworld was joined. It lasted almost four minutes.

The suit-to-suit intercoms were a gabble of shouts as Pertra's suddenly animated Thoughtworlders plunged into action. A few shots hissed in the first onslaught and a couple of Thinkers went down. Lineless, their corpses sailed up into the black yonder. There was no second onslaught because the first was enough to crush the attackers. 'We've numbers on our side,' thought Gormal, doing his bit. He snatched a humanoid figure as no-grav sent it away from Theeo, but not quickly enough for its liking or its health. Gormal pulled it down by the ankle, wrenched off the blast-pack, tossing it gaily towards infinity. With grim amusement, he repeated the trick twice more. He knew that at close quarters, numerical superiority plus grip-walk expertise would more than make up for lack of guns. He noticed ragged patches of strife around him: groups of Pertra's People singling out a lone attacker, disarming it if armed, relieving it of back-pack. Then off it went, another one gone. Occasionally, weapons flashed before they were ripped away. Thought-worlders died and drifted. A girl from F-block, dead, swayed with her foot caught in a grip as the press of bodies waved her this way and that.

The grapplers were in ponderous retreat. Obviously some-one had realised the requisite foothold wasn't going to be established. There wouldn't be sufficient troops left on Theeo in sufficient condition to operate the machines. There might not even be any. Very shortly, there were none. Roughly two dozen survivors managed to tear free and blast off. They dwindled like shrinking fireflies, heading for the seven ships. Bodies bobbled, bound for the eternal voyage. Some were dead already. All would be dead soon. Horrible visions filled Silver's head. This, too, could have been her fate. Seven ships cut trails of fire across space, defeated, and Derek stood alone, thinking about death.

Tynar didn't look like a genius: a seemingly ordinary adult male Tuahi, perhaps a bit abstracted around the eyes, but certainly not the kind of face to hint at a superb intellect such as that responsible for the Hypothesis.

'We wouldn't be here,' thought Arkon Vitch, 'if it weren't for him. None of us; either here in Theeo nor here in this office.' He gazed around Pertra's office, studying moods and postures: the Director himself, seated, strapped in, pensive; Gormal, a booted heavyweight, apparently even further

54

weighed down with worry; Dizzy Derek, up high in a corner, intoning a nursery rhyme; Silver, next to Vitch, expressionless; Cleo Rosa, pert and pretty, bootless, down the wall from Derek. 'And me, a devotee at the shrine of Tynar.' Vitch smiled thinly. A two-dimensional colour representation hardly constituted a shrine. After another glance at the Father of Thoughtworld, he scanned the thirteen inscriptions, picking out the language of Phorac III. All thirteen read the same:

TYNAR'S HYPOTHESIS: That thought, although immaterial (?), is, like light, measurably influenced by gravity. That the products of cellular brains, whether manifested as imagination, dreams, memory, ratiocination or intuition, would increase in potency and efficiency were the brain itself to be insulated totally against, or at least isolated as much as possible from the pernicious effects of gravity. That the thoughts, although immaterial (?), of all living organisms would achieve greater clarity and coherency by the removal of the organism into a place of artificially nullified gravity, or, until such is produced, into a region of space completely free from – or as completely free from as may be – all deleterious gravitational influence.

'Concise,' ruminated Vitch. 'And, by all that's impossible, correct!' He knew the question-marks were Tynar's own, included at his stubborn insistence. One of his unpublished ideas – some called it another flight of fantasy – was that thought might plausibly assume, after its generation in the brain, some solid or near-solid or perhaps so far unknown state on a different level of existence, a different plane, a different dimension, even quite simply in a different part of the charted physical universe.

He'd never attempted to formulate the idea, let alone prove it. He'd merely propounded it and challenged anyone to disprove it. No one had. But someone had proved the Hypothesis. Thoughtworld was its proof. Thought did benefit by being removed from the ponderous pull of gravity. Even here in the relative emptiness of Sector 17, Vitch could think more clearly, with fewer interruptions, fewer mental sidetrackings. And yet, if Theeo could get out into the Benlhaut Empire, or better still to the Void Regions . . . Arkon became aware of Gormal's deep voice, slightly irascible. 'We should do something!'

'But yes!' Pertra agreed amiably. 'But what? I call you all here for that, all you senior personnel. For suggestions.' His eyes, suddenly hard, turned on Gormal. 'Not for reiteration of the sentence in our every mind!'

'I'd say a formal complaint to the Empire,' Vitch ventured.

'Without proof? Ah, no! Without a single corpse to unsuit, to reveal an Imperial uniform – which Saril would claim to be a fake? No, no, Arkon. Our supply of corpses consists of twelve of our own, alas!'

'Well, a complaint might shake them up!'

'And might also shake the Emperor into hasty action. One can never predict the reactions of a member of the onhSaril Dynasty. Unless any sound idea is forthcoming, we must rely on the slow movements of "proper channels".'

Vitch detected a note of bitterness in Pertra's last two words. 'I assume you've set the wheels turning in the proper channels?'

'Naturally, my friend. The Thirteen will send authorised people to investigate – the sabotage, that is, not the larger issue. That's a Confed affair, too big for the Thirteen.'

Silver spoke for the first time. 'Couldn't we request the Thirteen to ask the Confed to increase the frequency of checks?'

'We could, my dear. In fact we have. I suggested an application for eight fly-pasts per month, doubling the frequency. But much depends on what forces the Confed can spare. And more depends, of course, on whether the Thirteen can . . . spare the money!'

Arkon again noted the bitterness in Pertra's voice. He felt bitter himself. 'God, they should be able to spare the money! The Thirteen exists purely to administer this place! Its funds were all collected to be used on us!'

'Precisely. Though I seriously doubt the Thirteen exists "purely", at all.' The Director's smile didn't reach his eyes. 'However, the suggestion has been made with firmness, if not with confidence in its being heeded.'

Words dripped hesitantly through Silver's mask. 'Shouldn't the Confed . . . well, at least take an interest in attempted theft within its jurisdiction?'

'It should and it does, child. Yet obviously it cannot spread its patrols widely enough to guard every object that might arouse the avarice of the unrighteous. Even a valuable object like Theeo. But rest assured, the Confed itself will investigate the greater atrocity, independently of the Thirteen. I was presumptuous enough to contact the Confed direct, on my own initiative, which may get me deposed,' Pertra's eyes smiled, 'to report the incident and also to, again on my own initiative, apply for those eight checks per month I suggested the Thirteen should request. I contacted Confed first.'

Vitch realised that the Director was a shrewd operator. If Confed Central granted his application, the Thirteen – whether or not they decided to make an identical application themselves, which they probably wouldn't – would be legally bound to honour the agreement and hand over the payment for it. They'd employed Pertra to run Theeo. If he considered more protection was needed because of the invasion, they had to back him. They had to abide by everything he'd been authorised to do, and done, while in office. They could throw him out afterwards, but his contract with Central would hold. They'd be stuck with it. Arkon revised his estimate. It hadn't been bitterness in Pertra's tone when he'd mentioned the Thirteen's ability to spare the money. It had been the grim amusement of an employee worsting, with perfect legality, an employer he plainly didn't like. Vitch admired him for it. He wasn't fond of the Thirteen, either.

'You understand? They have to make payment if the Confed can stretch Squadron 17 to eight checks in the month. Out I go, maybe. What suffers? Only me, a little. Not Thoughtworld.' Pertra resented the profits being gained from Theeo. In his estimation, such a boon to thought should be flung open to the entire Confed – no, even to Benlhaut, to all sentient creatures everywhere – at no cost whatsoever. It shouldn't be a private business enterprise, enriching only the Thirteen.

Cleo Rosa grip-slid down the wall. 'Couldn't Lundren help us? I read somewhere he's one of our most ardent fans. Perhaps he could pressurise Central into a massive investigation, not just the cursory one we can expect. A determined fight to uncover the truth. And then, if it's necessary – and with evidence, if they find any – drop a documented complaint right on Saril's conceited head!'

'Oh, but Confed will be thorough, not cursory,' Pertra explained. 'As for Lundren's being one of our most . . .'

'Vociferous admirers? I read the book, too.' Dizzy Derek stayed in his corner, but the flash of his eyes blazed down over everyone. 'Yes, he's certainly vociferous, but he's also resentful because he thinks he should be up here and he isn't!'

The Director looked bewildered. 'I'm not with you, Dizzy.'

'He put himself forward as a Thinker and then found he didn't meet the qualifications which he himself helped decide. Now if that's not a laugh, I'm not laughing!' Derek was laughing loudly. 'He tried to bend the rules and get himself through the Examination Board the easy way: via the side door, without taking exams he couldn't pass!'

'It's news to me.' Silver felt almost frightened by the uncontrollable quivering of Dizzy's body. It didn't seem to be altogether mirth.

'Although he had plenty of rule-bending accomplices, there was someone who refused to wilt before his tantrums! Although he close on had a fit, there was someone who stood in his way and defied him and met him word for word. There happened to be someone whose quiet obstinacy gathered a formidable group around him and opposed Lundren! Because . . .'

'That's enough!' interrupted Pertra, disturbed. 'Someone? Suppose you get hold of yourself and tell us who?' But Dizzy shut the world out and went back to his nursery rhyme.

Chapter Six

The sun disc curled over the rim of the world, bringing morning again to the countryside around Attica. The city itself slumbered in a hollow beside a broad slow river. Surrounding it were cultivated fields, vineyards and orchards. The dots of early traffic moved along the white ribbons of roads. Blossoms opened at the magical touch of daytime. New Athens looked very peaceful.

As star 17/LS6 climbed the sky, it watched workers toil, some singing. As it gradually ascended towards meridian, it watched Attica come alive, apparently tranquil. As it kissed the world with day, it seemed to bring a good day to a good world. But light breeds dark, and shadows crept over Peace Planet. Shade scurried across the land, as if to hint at a black presence among the bright colour, a diseased core in a fine fruit.

Joab Lundren sat at his cluttered desk and thought that sometimes one has to be cruel to be kind. He remembered many harsh acts, all unpalatable to an individual or a number of individuals, yet necessary for the smooth running of the State. Cruel to the few in order to be kind to the majority. A reasonable attitude, surely? He thought of himself as a tyrant, but in the original connotation rather than the erroneous new – an absolute ruler, *tyrannos*, meaning only 'lord' or 'master', the man best fitted for the position regardless of nepotism. He was the best fitted so he held the position. What could be fairer than that?

Admittedly his title was Prime Minister. Admittedly he sheltered what he considered his benevolent tyranny behind the mask of democracy. Yet he was still the master of New Athens, the power on Peace Planet. Therefore the term 'tyrant' suited him perfectly. He could hardly be held culpable for the fact that earlier tyrants had abused their authority and caused time to twist the meaning of the word.

Cruel to be kind. 'No!' The interruption came from inside him, the rebellious little corner of his mind, the insidious whisperer, whispering, 'Cruel? Oh yes, you're that! But kind? Never – except to yourself, which invariably involves cruelty to others!' He recognised it as an overdeveloped conscience, but this time he couldn't drown it. It mocked him like the feared enemy, death: 'You have abused your authority! Many times. Twisted yourself as the aeons have twisted a word. Power corrupts. You're living proof of it. Yes, you set out with wonderful intentions. You, a peaceful man, built a peaceful world of peaceful people. Beautiful! But a dream!'

He found himself arguing with himself, aloud. 'A dream?'

'Of course! Peace can't last! Not while the savage remains in us!' Lundren had to agree. Of all the races he'd seen, not a single one had pulled itself utterly clear of the jungle, up into enlightenment. Some vestige of violence always remained, underlying even the most brilliant gloss of civilisation.

'Why, the very universe itself isn't placid! Stars flame into death or freeze into death. Constant change, eternal turmoil. The Music of the Spheres is a raucous lack of harmony!' A lack of harmony? No, it couldn't be true. The universe pulsed with a perfect rhythm. A place for everything and everything in its place. He thought angrily: 'Order out of chaos ...'

'Order *out* of chaos? Rubbish! In the beginning there was chaos. Then a lesser chaos you choose to call order! But it's still chaos! Grinding down slowly to greater chaos, as it was in the beginning. Full circle!'

A question born of guilt scorched across Lundren's brain: when the Confed checked Theeo, did it also do a little periodical spying on New Athens? Could it have caught a forbidden glimpse of the EA?

'Another fact of nature: mostly, the top dog barks louder than he needs to, just to hear himself bark! And he bites, to prove his teeth are sharpest. You're the dog! Cruel to the few in order to be kind to the majority? How about cruelty to the whole population in order to be kind to one? To be kind to you! How about screening?'

Fading away, the whisperer left Lundren doubting his sanity. And doubting, too, the rectitude of what he'd done. He'd suppressed a truth, and he'd suppressed it if not by actual violence at least by invasion. He'd invaded the personality of every being on the planet, to benefit the planet. Benefit it? Yes, to maintain the myth of Peace Planet. And myth it was, today. Nothing more. Lundren visualised the screening machines, descendants of the ancient and clumsy electroencephalographs, but vastly refined. They not only recorded the brainwaves, they interpreted them, registered wave-frequencies and matched them against their source within the brain's tissue. The result was a chillingly accurate catalogue of emotions, desires, ambitions, and traits.

It wasn't mind-reading, but it was quite close. Not that he'd been much concerned with emotions, desires, or ambitions. He'd concentrated solely on what he'd called the aggression factor, and discovered, to his surprise, that it was present in every creature of every species. Which necessitated the establishment of a permissible aggression factor, covering both would-be settlers and visitors. Below it, you could come in. On or above it, no entry. Helpful in selecting Peace Planet's inhabitants – until 238!

Then Lundren visualised the other machines, the personality-invaders, vital since that awful year. They were descendants of the electroencephalographs, even more refined. They didn't break off at recording, they engineered change, such change as he wanted: psych-surgery!

One couldn't possibly stop a person seeing the EA. One couldn't mentally 'blind' a person or kill his curiosity, at least not without permanently altering the character. And Lundren sincerely wanted the people whom the earlier devices had selected, whom the earlier devices still selected. He simply didn't intend for them to mention the EA. Hence the refinements on refinements: obliterate a synapse here, bend a synapse there, divert a synapse somewhere else. Straightforward surgery, mind-manipulation, numbing the ability to speak of the secret EA. It worked on everybody apart from the natural immunes who saw things and took note of things. They were the ones who might talk, given the chance. The ones who had to be sacrificed to uphold Peace Planet's reputation, and Lundren's.

The whisperer had whispered truth. Joab Lundren's eyes glanced feverishly around the office, seeking somewhere to hide from the truth. He noticed:

> Another Athens shall arise,
> And to remoter time
> Bequeath . . .

And what had happened? Violence, bloodshed, and rebellion. The failed experiment of Peace Planet. The ruin of a man whose dream had become a nightmare, all day long and all through the night.

Lundren's star was at nadir. The tide of his hopes was at ebb. There was nowhere to hide in the office. There was nowhere to hide outside the office. The only hiding-place might be in the cool everlasting bosom of death. The thought of suicide brushed him and stayed for a long moment before departing, like the heavy shadow of a thundercloud loping slowly ahead of a straining wind. He dismissed it. Death could be an answer, a refuge, but not self-inflicted death. That was for lesser creatures, not for Joab Lundren. So, accept the truth! Clutch it tight, but never let it fly off into the ears of others! Never openly confess it! There could be no running away from truth, no salvation, only the empty comfort of silence.

Another salvation, although temporary, burst through the window in a storm of shattered glass. Part of the frame fell inwards noisily. Shouts rang from outside. Something rolled unevenly across the floor. A grenade! It was momentary salvation because it took his mind completely off the painful truth. Like a squashed ball, the steel bundle of concentrated destruction bounced over the carpet, past the desk, and rested with lethal impatience in a corner.

Lundren's chair crashed backwards as he leapt up, racing the other way. Panic flashed in his mind, lightened by inept humour. *'Now I won't need to bother!'* But it only served to increase the horror, by contrast. He reached the door and stopped. Somehow he knew the grenade was soon going to blow. He hadn't counted the seconds, and didn't even know how many seconds there should be before it exploded, but he just knew it was going to explode very soon. No time to get out! An itch ran down his back, the dreadful anticipation of imminent annihilation.

Lundren dived and the grenade blew. Metal tangled in the force of a vicious blast, furniture crumpled, glass erupted outwards, leaving behind glass which had already erupted inwards. Tumbling end over end, the desk came crazily across the carpet and banged the filing-cabinet behind which Lundren cowered. It knocked him into the corner but scarcely hurt him.

Seven seconds had passed since he'd first considered suicide. Shaken, he thought: 'They're getting ambitious!' Explosives were a speciality of the rebels lately, anywhere they could hamper Lundren's administration: Government offices, employment exchanges, EA stations, always with ample warnings, which had ensured no fatalities, just the odd cut. 'They've carved their initials on twigs and branches, crushed the juice out of a few leaves. And now they're after chopping the trunk right down dead!' Suddenly Joab Lundren felt very much afraid.

'The boy badly needs help,' thought Silver. She snatched a hold outside the door, pausing a moment with the button unpressed. It didn't seem odd to think of Dizzy as a boy. He had the advantage of several years over her, but still to her eyes he was a child in need of comfort and affection. She liked him and pitied him.

'Why the hesitation?' asked Vitch, booted, behind and below her.

'I'm not sure, Ark.' She kept her voice to a whisper. 'Only, are we really right to stick ourselves in his affairs?' Doubts touched her, despite her decision to offer whatever comfort she could.

'We don't intend to stick ourselves in; we intend to ask and offer. With friends, that's no invasion of privacy. It's friendship.' As he gestured for her to depress the stud, he won-

'dered why he'd accompanied her. Jealousy? Ridiculous! You simply couldn't feel jealous of Dizzy; it was impossible. He concluded that it must be a case of wherever Silver went, there he must go, too. Also he genuinely wanted to do what he could for Derek. 'Get it pressed, Sil.'

The memory of his violent quivering in Pertra's office, an alarming sight, overcame doubt. Yes, he had to be given comfort. She pressed the button and Derek's voice tore through the door, either surprised or frightened. 'Who is it?'

'Silver, Dizzy, and Ark. Can we talk?'

Sluggish seconds crawled by. Surely it wasn't such a difficult decision? A yes or no would suffice. Finally there was a commotion behind the door – it sounded like Derek unlocking the door and for some reason retreating – and he said, 'Come in'.

The panel slid away and revealed him backing quickly to the far wall. His eyes were wide and wary. He seemed relieved at seeing Vitch's boots, but suspicious of Silver's floating. One foot remained in contact with the wall, leg bent, as if he contemplated a fast take-off. Silver realised it had definitely been fear she'd heard in his voice. But why? Did his dark unreal inner-world contain evil phantoms? Until today, she'd always imagined it a land of fairies, colour and tiny elfin companions, a retreat from some dark outer reality.

Words weren't easy to find. 'Dizzy, we . . . myself and Ark . . . we wondered if . . . if . . . ' Then her words suddenly flowed in a torrent. 'Well, we could see you'd got something on your mind, perhaps an awful memory. Damn it, would it ease your burden to talk? If we can help, even just by listening.'

'Thanks, Silver; I appreciate that. You too, Arkon.' He spoke with close control, but the suspicion lingered. 'I have things on my mind, yes. Who hasn't? Yet I'm lucky.' He brightened. 'I've less mind than most folks, you see. Less room for the things on it. That's a blessing.'

'Seriously, Derek . . . '

'Seriously, Silver, seriousness is harmful in large doses. Too much profound thinking hurts! So laugh! Temper

64

gravity . . . ' He chuckled at the pun. Saliva-globs hung on air. 'Temper gravity with . . . ' Derek paused, then sung his nursery rhyme for fully two minutes, to the amazement of Silver and Arkon, ' . . . levity!' He sung it again, a shorter version.

'Is he real?' thought Silver. 'Is the idiocy real? Or an act?' She knew it was real. It was maintained too immaculately to be an act. And supposing it were an act, why the sudden unpredictable surges into brief sanity? Obviously something had shocked him into his present state.

The door buzzed. Derek didn't know, but he snapped into rigidity. He hazarded a shrewd guess and decided someone must be outside, wanting to come in. Could he trust his two visitors? Could they have both been involved in the attack on him? Did another potential murderer even now wait in the corridor? He didn't fancy his chances much against three. His voice trundled from his mouth, reluctant and tremulous. 'Who is it?'

'A humble friend, Dizzy. May he enter?'

Two in boots and one floater, Derek calculated. Better than two floaters and one in boots. He'd risk it. Pertra wouldn't have progressed beyond the boot stage yet. 'Yes. Walk in.'

Pertra floated in. 'I learn, I grow proficient!' He sailed around the room clumsily but happily, and noticed the other two. 'Ah, company! I don't intrude?'

'No, no, you're welcome!' ('I hope!'). 'Can I help you?'

'I rather believed the contrary. That I could aid you, Dizzy. I often read anguish in the heart of a person. I read it in yours. I thought, perhaps, a sympathetic ear . . . '

'That's kind of you. I'm surrounded by friends.' Friends? He could only pray they were friends. If they were all in league – no, that didn't bear thinking about! Suddenly he spotted consolation: if any one or two of them had his destruction in mind, the presence of the third should restrain him or her or them. But if all three were together . . .

'A sympathetic ear, a sympathetic brain. A receptacle into which to pour troubles, to lessen them by the sharing.' Pertra glanced at Vitch and Silver. 'We are all here together for the same purpose?' Derek's heart thundered.

'Ah, good!' The affirmative pleased the Director. 'Well, Dizzy, if we may be your three receptacles, so be it! If we presume too much, merely show us the door.'

'It's there.' Derek pointed.

'You wish us to go?'

He giggled. 'No, no, of course not!' Derek lied. 'Just trying to be helpful.'

'Ah, yes, I follow. Most hilarious.' Pertra managed to smile. 'I noticed earlier your tension on speaking of . . . someone, as I notice it now on my mentioning it. A mind-doctor would urge you to talk of this enigmatical someone, to unload, to rid your system of the majority of its injurious associations, partially to exorcise you of this someone.'

Derek thought: 'How can you exorcise yourself of *that* someone?'

'Perhaps under hypnosis, for which we here aren't equipped. Still even without it . . . ' Pertra stopped; Dizzy's blank gaze made it clear he wasn't getting anywhere. Pertra tried the tactic of trying to take Dizzy's side: 'Now you say this someone thwarted Lundren? A laudable action, that! Why not talk about it?' This time Pertra felt a flush of anger as Dizzy again sought sanctuary in his nursery rhyme. The Director turned to Arkon and Silver and shrugged. His expression said, 'What can one do? How can one help the helpless who refuse to be helped?'

A Thinker clumped along the outer corridor, reciting poetry. 'Gormal,' Silver observed absently. Derek stiffened, staring at the door. His previously empty face now filled with sudden apprehension. He seemed to be listening for the buzzer but not wanting to hear it. A barely audible word escaped his pale lips: 'Four?' The clumping poet passed on and Dizzy relaxed.

Pertra tried another method. He air-trod closer to Derek and asked gently, 'A vacation? Would it ease you? Anywhere you like, for an indefinite period?' But he didn't expect any response. Thoughtworlders often took a month or so out to visit home, or any place they chose. New Athens was popular because of the apparent placidity of life there, although most Thinkers suspected shadow beneath the superficial shine. Also the planet was popular with the

Thirteen as a holiday spot for Theeo's staff as it was the closest and so it cost less to ship them there. Pertra had taken the trouble to check on various aspects of vacation. He knew Derek had plenty of time due to him, as did everyone in A-block. They were conscientious workers and only used a little of their leave. They'd all visited New Athens and brought back casual reports contradicting the planet's Confed-wide image.

'A couple of months at home, Derek?' Pertra suggested. 'I can stretch the length of time to any reasonable period, especially if your health . . . ' Again he stopped. It might be a touchy subject. And anyway, wherever he went, Derek would most likely take with him the brain-shadow tied up inside his head. Maybe he was beyond help. He seemed to be.

While Pertra pondered, Derek stayed in his leg-flexed pose, set for instant flight from some enemy evidently trapped in his mind. His muscles were tight, poised for haste, but he was still singing. When he stopped, silence fell except for steady breathing. Animation suddenly sparkled in his eyes, but he spoke with more confidence than he felt. 'Thanks, Pertra; I see you've my welfare at heart. But I'll face it out. Just remember I'm a trifle abnormal and then everything I do will appear quite normal . . . for me.'

'Strange advice, but I grasp it. However, please reconsider: perhaps a while resting; a month in pleasant fields and woods. New Athens perhaps?'

'You're joking! Pleasant? The countryside's nice, yes, but have you forgotten 238?'

'When Lundren nearly had Peace Planet's levy-exemption rescinded on account of internal squabbles? I recall it, but that's over.'

'*That's* over,' Derek agreed. '238's over. Yet when a year passes, it doesn't die. It lives on in future years by affecting them.' He paused for his meaning to sink in. Nobody argued. Rumours drifted from Peace Planet: rumours of small acts of rebellion against the government. 'Look, Sciri, give up trying. I may be my worst enemy, yet I'm still the closest friend I've got. Not that I'm knocking your efforts, you three. It's just that some things a man has to square up to alone. Conquer them alone. Or not conquer them. Only it has to be alone.'

'The philosophy of the lonely,' thought Pertra. 'Or the loner. There's a difference. Who am I to tell him he's wrong, when I believe he could be right?' Aloud he said: 'I understand, Dizzy. I did no more than what I mistakenly conceived of as my duty. As a fellow-creature, not a Director. Regrettably I overstepped the mark.'

'Not at all!' Derek sounded sincere. 'In friendship, you only overstep the mark in one way: by going a tiny bit too far, irreversibly, and becoming an enemy.' His unusual coherence kept the others quiet. 'As a Director, you're a good one. They'll kick you out soon, of course; you're too much of an individual thinker to be allowed to last long. Like Dat.'

'Like what?' asked Pertra, misunderstanding him.

'Like Dat. Burl Dat, our last Director but one but one but one. Four Directors ago. He was an individual, too, so he had to go. Except he denied them the pleasure of sacking him. He resigned; driven to it, mind, but he played his card before they could play theirs. A fine person!'

Arkon Vitch seconded Derek's opinion. 'That's true. I remember Dat. Quietly spoken, easy-going, but stern when necessary. Unfortunately he was forced to bow out with dignity. There were arguments.'

'Yes, and remember who he argued with!' Emotion scorched in Dizzy's eyes. His voice rang with abrupt vehemence. Then he withdrew into his shell. Hot emotion sputtered into nothing but an unseeing stare. His lips closed in introspective, and retrospective silence. He seemed to have burned up all his conversational energy for the moment. Right now, he hadn't even the energy to be scared.

Outside, they moved along the corridor and then stopped. Vitch stepped to the side of the walkway, half-on, half-off. His heels, in contact with plastic, lifted; his soles remained magnetised to the metal. It was a peculiar sensation. He bobbed himself slowly up and down, like a leaf in a wind which couldn't decide whether to drop him or keep him.

The Director and Silver held handholds, out of the way of traffic.

An alarm shrilled and Thoughtworld juddered. 'Must have been a big one,' Silver said through her mask. Electronic hums raced throbbingly in the walls as command impulses were sent out. Once more a shudder shook Theeo, but more gently, and controlled. Up on the surface, stabilising blasts directed by computer set the planetoid back where it belonged and cut out its incipient spin. The alarms only shrieked at strikes by very large meteorites, in the unlikely event of their being large enough to have pierced the crust.

The shrilling ceased. 'As we were. No hole.' Pertra mastered his relief and spoke evenly. 'That lad worries me. There's a weight on his soul and he doesn't know how to raise it.'

'Perhaps he does,' murmured Silver, 'but lacks the strength to do it. Or possesses the strength, but needs to raise it gradually.'

'Ah, but is it a question of strength? We offered him that, in abundance. It could go deeper than any of us realise.'

'As Derek does,' Vitch put in cryptically. 'Certainly he's verging on the imbecilic, but with those occasional flashes of perspicacity, profundity, and even downright sanity, he can't be an utter imbecile. You don't ascend to Thoughtworld without passing rigorous and extremely selective tests.'

'Unless your name's Lundren! And you don't have a mysterious someone opposing you.' Pertra became solemn. 'Speaking of profundity, and I quote: "When a year passes, it doesn't die. It lives on in future years by affecting them". A point one would be foolish to contest. A point moreover, made by a distorted mind. No, he's not an utter imbecile!'

'He may be no kind of imbecile at all.' Although she didn't mention it, Silver remembered overhearing a group of students talking about Derek. An argument as to his right to be in Theeo had been terminated by forceful words she'd never forgotten: 'He's such an idiot he must be a genius!' It had a ring of truth to it, she felt. 'And he knows which way the scales are tipping on New Athens. That's more than most of the Athenians know!'

'Your score, Sil. 238's bound to return.' Arkon bobbed.

'Not by any time-twist, simply because plain old-fashioned psychology says it must. No student of the behaviour of . . . intelligent? . . . species would argue against that. 238 will happen again, just as it happened the first time, and for an identical reason: inevitability.'

In Pertra's brain clanged chains of concurrence, a concatenation forged of link upon link of sound logic. Peace Planet had been ripe for internal explosion long before 238. That year had been nothing more than the time when a smouldering fuse called Lev Merrin had ignited a deadly inflammable substance called unrest.

Since its colonisation in 197, New Athens had seemed to be paradise. At least, no hint of dissent had seeped out. But Pertra had learned a lesson from studying history: tranquillity is finite, not eternal. He had every respect for the opinions and ideals of the original settlers – the pacifists, the discontented – yet he realised they'd been chasing dreams. Thinking they'd found heaven, they'd found only temporary shelter from hell. 238's violence *had* to come. In the very nature of things, and of people, it couldn't be avoided.

'It was an inevitable occurrence,' he assented. 'We're little better than machines; worse, in many respects! Who programmed us, I don't know; I prefer not to dwell upon it too much, since I feel myself shrinking with every metaphysical or theological question left unanswered. And how many *are* answered satisfactorily?' He made a despairing gesture. 'We react to stimuli, machine-like – although in a complex manner, tangled by emotions – and I occasionally think the Almighty Programmer has Himself a good laugh at our conceits.'

Pertra waited for someone else to take up the topic. No one did. 'I said machines? I could have said bombs! In our machine-guise, we come up with the same reaction to a whole spectrum of stimuli: violence. We live by it and die from it sometimes. As bombs, all we need is a depressed plunger or a flame applied. Maybe even the Great Almighty Programmer detonates us from afar now and then for some vast joke we're too tiny to appreciate. And often too dead!'

'What surprises me,' said Vitch, 'is that it took so long to

70

come to a head. Okay, Lundren's original lot were probably a fine crowd in theory. But they had their own self-styled titles to live up to; hence wholesale repression of instincts and widespread lie-living. Then they'd have children. More people, more repression, more savagery looking for an out-let. The marvel is, it took forty-one years to spark off!'

'Ah, if we could suppress the ugly instincts totally then we'd have advanced. Next step: eradicating them totally.' Pertra smiled at his own daydreaming. 'I ramble. We can only lament the ferocity of rebel and non-rebel alike. The desire to overturn authority in the former, the vicious brutality with which the latter stamped out the insurrection. A pity from start to finish, whenever that is!'

Silver said succinctly, 'So much for screening!'

'Indeed, my dear! The boasted screening. The aggression factor. I wonder what Lundren's is?'

'High!' The monosyllable lashed from Vitch, a word-whip. 'There was a little-publicised libel action some years ago. Lundren as plaintiff, a talented young poet as defendant. Remember it?' He received two negatives. 'Well, the kid must have had a grievance and tore Lundren to shreds with a single short poem. No subtlety, or else the youngster just didn't care. Whoever it was − I don't recall any name, even species − the kid called the work *JL: An Attack!* And it *was* an attack! I read a copy before the unsold ones were de-stroyed after the hearing. It was so flagrantly libellous that the case was a formality. The poem referred to JL's face: supposedly hard as a rock, apart from his public smile. All teeth. It slammed him for a number of rule-bends, and said he made the law a weapon against enemies and a shield for himself. I only recollect a couple of lines:

"I rate the man a hateful man. I urge you not to trust his
"Adamantine face and his Rhadamantine justice"

plus plenty more, even harsher. Anyway, Lundren went in with the maximum legal aggression.' Vitch smiled coldly and paused to let the point register. 'The suit completely broke the kid financially. Lundren had ways of seeing to that.'

A sudden thought occurred to Pertra. 'Finance, that is

71

nothing. Did Lundren also break the youngster's spirit?'

Arkon Vitch spread his hands. 'I've no idea.'

Dizzy Derek hung in spare-time Think, spare-time Thinking. It was A-block's pet project, extra-schedule; not quite secret, but not widely talked about with outsiders. It had to be done in A-block. It was far too vast for anyone with lesser abilities than Theeo's top five. Often it seemed far too vast for them, because it was extremely ambitious and possibly presumptious.

They wanted to crack the universe wide open and come to terms with God, supposing He existed. They wanted to unravel primordial cosmic secrets, delve into the universe's mysteries, then surface with an excited cry of 'Truth!' They wanted the Supreme Being, face to face, with all His works and reasons.

'That's all,' thought Derek, descending momentarily to ordinary Think from the intoxicating realms of extra-ordinary Think. 'Only how do you find what your instincts tell you isn't there to be found?' It was like playing hide-and-seek without any real faith that someone was actually hiding; the most enormous of playgrounds in which to search, but you just couldn't be positive you'd uncover the other player even if you looked in the right place. The other player might be nothing but part of your imagination. Or he might be such a preternaturally skilful adversary that he could prevent your seeing him even if you stared right at him.

As for the secrets, what if they didn't appear to be secrets? What if the complex seemed simple, the simple complex? The adversary – if there was one – could be an expert in subtle camouflage. You could waste the entire game search-ing in the wrong places for the wrong things, with Truth screaming its presence unheard under your ignorant nose.

Suppose the Big Bang theory could be refuted as easily as the statement $1 + 1 = 3$? Suppose the Steady State hypothesis could be torn apart with equal ease. Suppose the cosmos could be declared finite or infinite with as little diffi-culty as declaring whether or not $2 + 2 = 4$?

Derek pondered on the enormity of the task. Still, it had

to be done. Intelligent creatures had never before possessed such an aid to cerebration as Theeo. No matter how slender the chances of success, no matter how slim the chances of even fractional success, it had to be tried. Curiosity dictated it. A-block's Thinkers spent as much leisure-time as they could at it: probing the universe, thought-fingers reaching into black depths that could contain a partial answer or a total madness; rolling questions around their heads, Thinking about that which often seemed to defy thought; comparing notes, exchanging ideas, arguing and discussing, all the while trying to snatch the answers to questions they could scarcely set down sensibly.

Progress was always slow, except when it stopped altogether. They realised they could have taken on too much, but they stuck to it with tenacity bordering on obstinacy. They designated it, with mental capital letters, The Breakthrough, yet what they were hoping to break through they couldn't definitely say. Space? Time? Religion? Metaphysics? Ignorance, most likely. Occasionally they seemed to be close, but . . . The shot was closer. It zipped past Dizzy's head, whining. Simultaneously he heard a sharp crack. He turned quickly, looking for the enemy. A door was closing. He thought: 'It missed, I'm safe,' and then realised he wasn't. He was in a no-grav room with a bullet that wouldn't stop zipping for a long while. Unless something absorbed it, it would not cease its flight for a good many days. He didn't even want to stay with it for a minute.

It sang around the room, wall to wall, to floor to ceiling, slanting off in wild lethal ricochets. He knew he could predict its course right down to the time it finally lost its momentum if he could spare thought for the problem and if it didn't lose its inertia in some absorbent body such as his own. His grasp of mathematics was brilliant. His grasp on life at the moment appeared to be tenuous, precarious and insecure.

There were two exits, not counting death. To reach either of the two, all Dizzy had to do was get through the unpredictable criss-cross pattern of a hungry bullet – an up-and-down, side-to-side, wall-to-wall, ceiling-to-anywhere network of potential murder. It looked difficult. No wonder the attacker hadn't bothered with a second shot. A first shot, even a complete miss, could eventually hit.

Both exits were closed. No problem there, they'd open at the touch of a finger. Which still left a big problem: how to get the finger across the room without losing finger, arm, maybe life? Derek pondered, while the bullet continued its course with no visible decrease in its velocity. Once it ripped his shirt. Twice it warmed his face. If it happened to home in on a killing course, there'd be no dodging it. A door opened and a robot whirred in, passing through. It had every right to do so, since the 'In Think' panel wasn't lit up outside during Breakthrough sessions. A Thinker could hardly divert a busy robot because he was himself only working on a diversion, not a Thirteen-sent Think. In the case of official Think, robots and people alike simply had to find another route to their destinations.

Dizzy resented the machine's presence. If he had to die, he'd rather die alone, or at least with living companions. It seemed vaguely undignified and ignominious to be killed in front of a robot, although, of course, it wasn't sufficiently sensitive to even notice him, dead or alive. It continued on its errand mechanically, then flopped into inactivity with a bullet in its power-pack. After relief, fear caught up with Derek, as exquisitely and intimately frightful as a ghost's kiss. 'A ghost's kiss?' Vile memory hit him out of the lost years. He fainted.

As Pertra sat pensively at his desk, Dizzy Derek's enigmatic words echoed in his ears: 'Yes, and remember who he argued with!' He'd named no names, but he'd clearly intimated that the reasons behind Burl Dat's abrupt departure from Theeo were worth investigating. There'd been an unaccustomed fire burning in Derek's normally dull eyes, a passion in his speech rarely evinced. These two things in themselves warranted a check on the last days of Dat.

'Also I'm curious,' mused Pertra, decisively standing up and booting his way to the filing-cabinets. He didn't know exactly what an investigation would turn up, yet obviously the exit of ex-Director Burl Dat must be closely examined.

'I might learn something to make my own tenure less uncertain. A selfish motive, but . . . '

In the fourth drawer he opened, Pertra found a copyspool of Dat's last official communication from Thoughtworld. The Director pulled it from its clip, lifting out a portable playback. Strapped in again, he set the machine on his desk and inserted the spool. He caught Dat in midsentence: ' . . . in view of the many previous conflicts in policy, I feel I can no longer hold this position with an untroubled conscience. It seems to me that my term of usefulness has expired. These latest differences, especially those with Prime Minister Lundren . . . '

Pertra jerked forward, made the words repeat themselves. He'd heard right first time. Superfluously, he listened through till the end. ' . . . have made concrete a decision which has been forming in my mind for some time, throughout all the political turbulence haunting this post; and haunting it unnecessarily and most unfairly, in my opinion, since I believe politics and self-interest should not be allowed to interfere with the remarkable work being carried out by the excellent team here. Being no hypocrite, I have no intention of remaining in this intolerable situation solely for the prestige involved. Prestige I can live without, self-respect I cannot. Nor shall I wait passively until an enemy has pulled the job out from underneath me by force. The only course open to me is to regretfully offer my resignation.'

The Director switched off. He didn't need to check further. Dat's resignation had been accepted, no doubt about that, and probably no doubt about who'd made sure the Thirteen accepted it! I'd like to have met you, he thought, replacing spool and playback. He pictured Dat as a creature of integrity, most likely an ideal Director. But he'd tackled Lundren and Lundren was plainly not a safe man to tackle. 'You've opened my eyes, Derek. Thank you. Only why the fire in your own?'

Chapter Seven

Vitch discovered Derek in free-fall, quite free but not falling anywhere. He was a horizontal unconsciousness, rotating slowly on its head-to-foot axis. Nothing external indicated his shocked withdrawal into a sombre half-world where the kissing spectres of the lost years couldn't torment him. He looked peaceful and unhurt.

'Derek?' Vitch received no answer, but he wasn't alarmed. Dizzy had gone to sleep on the job before, many a time. 'Derek?' He repeated the name, then louder still.

No response. Buckles clicked as Vitch kicked himself briskly out of his boots. They remained on the walkway as he steered Dizzy and steadied his senseless turning. A rip in his shirt puzzled him. Derek's face was pale, his breathing shallow but no cause for worry. It could be simple slumber, despite the pallor.

Vitch noticed the robot. It stood inert, upright, feet magnetised to the walkway. The manufactured body rocked gently, erect, as from some blow. There was a large cavity in its chest. Vitch guessed it was pack-explosion. He re-booted and examined the robot's damage. Exploding power-packs weren't rare. They happened now and then. Robots malfunctioned, as well as people. He wasn't too concerned about the damage. His fingers ran delicately over the chest: curled-back metal and plastic, a hole, the wreckage of the power-pack, with a bullet embedded in it!

Arkon looked up: a stationary and pale Derek. Arkon looked down: a useless robot, shot. Any connection? Assume Dizzy shot the robot. Okay, so what had stunned Dizzy? Or was he asleep? Either way, where was the gun?

76

And if Dizzy hadn't used it, who had? And if Dizzy had used it, why had he used it? Robots were perfectly harmless, no threat. Even if he'd imagined danger from one, surely he'd brain enough to realise he could easily outpace it and effect a non-violent escape? Maybe he hasn't brain enough? Perhaps he'd expected it to follow him wherever he went, a hunt to the death, so he'd shot it? But that was stretching idiocy, even for Dizzy.

Arkon scratched his head, bemused. Then he stared up, startled. Dizzy was rotating again and muttering disquietingly about ghosts — ghosts with soft lips, kissing people. It didn't make sense. Vitch began to feel strangely nervous. The words had such an uncanny ring, bizarre words dredged up from a macabre fancy. They almost scared him.

He unbooted, went to Derek and shook him thoroughly. 'Dizzy! Get hold of yourself! Calm down and . . . oh, hell!' He swore at the stupidity of it. It might have been laughable if it hadn't been so tragic and pathetic. Derek had got hold of himself, as commanded. His arms were wrapped tight around his chest, as if embracing an invisible lover. 'Arkon?'

'Yes, yes, it's me! Now what happened? I found you out cold.'

'Cold!' screamed Derek, and he gave the syllable such a freezing, frightening quality that Vitch suddenly did feel cold and chilled with a nameless fear. 'Cold, yes. They kiss, Arkon. Though dead.'

Vitch decided to try levity. 'You mean vampires?'

'Vampires?' An abrupt broken laugh nearly broke Arkon's grip on the fear. It came close to bursting out as unadulterated terror. Derek's insane laugh fell to an insane titter. 'Not vampires, Arkon. Ghosts. With lips that kiss!'

Uncertainty ran through Vitch's shaken mind. Was all this nonsense just a raving of an unbalanced mentality? Or did it have a foundation in reality, way back? Did the dreadful references to ghosts, ghostly kisses, ghosts with soft lips, point to some unspeakable horror in Dizzy's past — a colossal shock, in some inexplicable manner involving ghosts and lips and kisses, which had tripped him over an awful brink?

'Like this.' Derek moved his arms, tightened his embrace

77

on himself or the invisible lover. 'Just like this . . . arms round me . . . she held me . . . she . . . she . . . she . . . ' He was shrieking now, a repetitive chant. Arkon slapped him flat-handed across the face and Derek's fist replied with a hard lunge to the stomach. Vitch gasped, breathless. The return blow, so quick and expert, had surprised him. The slap had sobered Derek. They glared at each other in hostile stupe-faction – Dizzy because a veil had lifted, Arkon because he hadn't expected such obvious experience and fast reflexes in Dizzy.

'I'm sorry, Derek. It seemed necessary.'

'I'm sorry too, Ark. Only don't try it again, will you?'

And Arkon Vitch realised he wouldn't dare. To salvage a little pride, he said. 'No. Unless it's necessary again.' But he didn't believe it. 'God! There's lightning in the man. Just waiting to strike. I hope I'm not around when it does.' Warily, he changed a touchy subject. 'That robot. What went wrong?'

'It got shot.' Derek saw the other's eyebrows raise inter-rogatively, and he wondered how much he could disclose. He didn't want to mention the attempts on his life. Even if he could be sure of being believed, his solitary nature wouldn't allow it. He'd see it through alone. He thought that maybe the best policy was to act dumb. He wondered if Vitch already knew what had gone wrong: the robot had been deactivated instead of the Thinker. From the attacker's point of view, that was what had really gone wrong. Vitch could have been the attacker. Derek acted dumb.

'Well? What went wrong?' Arkon persisted.

'I . . . ' Derek paused, swallowing exasperation at Vitch's doggedness. 'I was in Think when somebody opened the door and let the machine have it. A practical joke, probably.'

'Not very practical.' Arkon showed no sign of credulity or otherwise. Derek hadn't expected much. If he were the would-be killer, he'd consider his every word and action as closly as Dizzy intended to consider his own. 'More sabotage, do you think?' asked Vitch.

'Doubtful. Just one robot? It'd be the pettiest yet.' A frown saw ephemeral life on Dizzy's face, the shadow of his uncertainty. He sighed, blinked and quoted, for no apparent reason:

> 'Arms of marble, eyes of sapphire,
> 'Death-glaze filming over;
> 'And I weep beside the corpse
> 'Of her, my new-dead lover.'

Then he added quietly, 'That's from a verse whose name I can't remember. Very appropriate. I forgot who wrote it.'

A taut wire of memory twanged in Arkon; something somebody had said recently, some conversation between himself and Pertra. But he couldn't exactly place it, couldn't precisely trace it. He mentally recited Tynar's Hypothesis, then thought: 'Here's Vitch's corollary: That the failings of cellular brains, such as delusions, madness, neuroses, obsessions and hatred, must also increase in potency in no-grav.' In Derek's case, it seemed totally irrefragable.

Lundren asked impatiently, 'What do you want?' The visiplate showed his unsmiling face, age-lines crossing temper-grooves, a forbidding mask concealing a calculating brain.

Nervously, the communicant chewed a lower lip, wondering how to impart his news. 'I tried again. Missed again.' It wasn't easy to say.

'Two shots, two failures!' From Lundren's tight mouth shot a foul oath. 'Have I got to come up there and do it myself?'

There was a sharp intake of breath, another bite at the lip to chop off hasty speech. Words formed which must never be said: 'You? Come up here? That'll be the day, when you do the dirty work! And you're not fit to be here! Not as a Thinker, anyway, because you're short of what it takes and somebody wouldn't let you bludgeon your way through!' But to speak thus would be to invite bad trouble, so the words had to remain a burden in the head, an impossible ambition. They hurt.

Lundren waited, a set of cruel features, for something to be said.

'Is it . . . ?' A pause followed, a searching for courage. 'I mean, is it necessary? Derek. His murder.' ('Him being who he is? Of course it is! Yet . . . ')

'You aren't questioning my decisions, are you?' Lundren inquired with dangerous politeness. With sadistic pleasure he watched the head shake, the cheeks redden with bitter humiliation. He derived an hour's enjoyment from a few seconds of embarrassment and fear. 'That's good. I wouldn't be happy if you did.' His laugh had no humour in it, only malice. 'Let's hope you're more fortunate next time. For your sake.'

'But . . . '

'Do it!' Immediately, the screen went blank.

He didn't like his temporary office. It was too small for a big man. Lundren clenched his fists and squeezed hard, as if his impatience would speed up repairs. His original office was untenable: broken furniture, smashed windows and fire damage. Ominously, the framed piece of archaic poesy had been completely incinerated.

' "Another Athens," ' he thought gloomily. ' "And leave, if nought so bright may live . . . " ' Well, his particular Athens could have been bright, but nowadays the glitter had gone. 'If nought so bright may live?' Yes, it seemed New Athens might not be permitted to live; Lundren had to admit it. Though exactly why should it be forced into extinction? 'Because of the rebels,' Lundren told himself wordlessly. 'Because they've darkened the shine I put on Peace Planet, with their sedition and dissatisfaction!'

The insidious whisperer dared to disagree. It whispered from the inside of his head to the inside of his head, 'Arrant sophistry! Delusion! The culprit is governmental corruption, the reason for the dissatisfaction. The culprit is none other than . . . '

He slammed a hand on to the desk. The sudden sound successfully drew his treacherous deep-mind from thoughts of sedition. He managed to think once more precisely as he wished to think, about the hated rebels. Early morning sunlight cascaded in crystalline brilliance through the windows as black clouds of stormy loathing welled up in his brain: loathing of the disease started, or at least made more virulent, by Lev Merrin, then cured with surgical expertise by the loyal element in 238.

'Cured?' asked a hidden whisper. 'Then how is it that it's even more virulent today? Surgical expertise? I doubt it! Surgical detachment, yes. But without anaesthetic, with no attempt to alleviate the pain. Say, rather, with the expert brutality of a crazed surgeon!' Trembling, Lundren could almost feel his mind shattering, his sanity crumbling, his personality separating. He was too frightened and pre-occupied to hear the noise outside in the courtyard. It rose to a great muttering from many throats: cries of surprise, fury and shock. But he didn't hear it.

In his head roared worry upon worry: the threat posed by Dizzy Derek, if it were a threat and not coincidence; the inefficient efforts to kill the fool, up high in Theeo; the anxiety over an indispensable EA. If one of the black-market munitions organisations were to hint at certain dealings . . . The intercom bell rang stridently. He lifted the receiver. 'Yes?'

'Out in the courtyard, sir. I think you ought to come down.'

'You do, do you? Isn't it more to the point what I think?'

A voice stammered, 'Well . . . yes, sir. Of course, but . . . '

'Shut up! What's the trouble?'

'The rebels, sir. Perhaps their boldest strike to date. Really, sir, you ought to see for yourself. Their boldest . . . '

'Boldest? Probably their third-boldest,' Lundren thought, remembering 238 and the grenade. 'I'll be down.' Grimly, he left the office, strode into a courtyard full of chattering people, and stopped short with a gasp when he saw it. It was definitely bold: a tall memorial stone set firmly in the ground, headed by the legend 'Our Glorious Dead'. On the slab, intricately and carefully carved, were names, names that upset Lundren's sleep, arranged in an erroneous though impressive genealogy:

L. MERRIN

K. MERRIN   R. MERRIN

10,000 GOOD MEN, WHO DID NOT DIE IN VAIN

———————————THE LIVING ONES———————————

100,000 GOOD MEN (AND GROWING), WHO WILL NOT
FIGHT IN VAIN

WE'RE WAITING

THE WRITING'S ON THE WALL, LUNDREN

'Devil take the bastards!' he hissed hoarsely. With bitter reluctance, he admired their audacity, courage and planning. Their timing must have been perfect, between patrols. Their work rate could have been nothing less than phenomenal; the hole dug, the stone planted, over the wall and away, all inside thirty seconds at the most. But his admiration didn't last long. He glanced in sullen fury at the top three names, the triumvirate in command of the insurgents until 238, when they'd all been killed. It gave him no comfort to know the supposed family-tree bore no relevance to lineal descent, matrimonial connections or true births. It was only a well-designed reconstruction of the rebels' defunct hierarchy.

According to the genealogy, Lev Merrin was the sire of his own father and uncle. Karl Merrin and his brother had between them borne '10,000 Good Men' who, in their turn, had borne 100,000 more, still alive, still waiting. But despite the familial inaccuracies, the point had been very forcefully made. Lundren's gaze fell to the bottom line: 'The Writing's on the Wall, Lundren'. Instinctively, he whirled round, gaped in astonishment and cool horror. The writing was indeed on the wall, literally, in painted letters a yard high: 'You've Had a Long Day, Lundren. Prepare for Night'. Mated with the slab it could have only one meaning. It was an elaborate, glyphic, coloured announcement of his forthcoming death – if they could pull it off. He began to feel they could.

Abruptly, he shook with agonising regret at a single fact: the rebel who'd thrown the grenade had been shot as soon as he'd flung it. 'A pity,' he mused. 'It was too fast, not sufficiently drawn-out.' Also the rebel could have served a better purpose alive than dead: a trial with planetwide news coverage and a public execution. It wouldn't help Peace Planet's image around the Confed, but it ought to make a few vacillating minds think twice at home. He realised New Athens was slipping out of his hands, slithering from his control. Even the religious factions were resorting to violence instead of propaganda these days. There'd been open confrontations between the Children of Peace and the Imminent Millennium Order within the past week; not an exchange of pamphlets and arguments, but a bloody exchange of blows.

He thought cynically: 'If the Children of Peace can't be peaceful, what price the Imminent Millennium?' It almost amused him, in a cold mirthless sort of way. A developing chuckle froze dead deep down inside him, stillborn. Against his will, his eyes held steady on the painted warning: 'You've Had a Long Day, Lundren. Prepare for Night'.

'If only you were human,' said Cleo Rosa wistfully. She gazed at Gormal with a respect as immense as his gigantic frame. 'We have so much in common. Soul mates.' Her beautiful dark eyes sparkled with a love beyond mere sexuality. Her lack of surprise at the emotion surprised her. 'Yet no matter how close you get to someone . . .'

He sensed her difficulty and eased her out of it. 'Alien. That's the word. Don't be afraid to say it. You're alien also, to me.'

'Alien. Thank you. No matter how close – talking, exchanging experiences, ambitions, tastes – there's always an inter-species gulf, not only of body but of mind. I mean, we're as close as we can ever be physically, because . . .'

'I'd squash you. Not to mention splitting you in half.'

Her cheeks flushed with quick anger. 'I'm being serious!'

'So am I. Completely. You mistake alien seriousness for the coarse humour it would have been from a human tongue. Never forget, different races are different. This is the first lesson on the obstacle-filled road to concord.'

'Lesson learned,' she replied meekly. She rested, foetal, in the air. In Gormal's personal rooms, she was uncomfortable on account of his smell, but comfortable on account of his presence: huge, reassuring, philosophic and different. She felt relaxed in his company. 'I wish . . . ' Her voice whipped off into a scream. Nothing was normal any more. Everything was wrong.

There was gravity. She fell out of nothing, crashed into something: the floor, unyielding. It smacked her as though with sentient savagery, clubbed her, knocked her. She finished up lying very still – while Theeo spun! Improbably, appallingly, impossibly – except for the whirling fact which proved the possibility, the actuality – Thoughtworld was spinning.

Shouting incoherently, Gormal rolled across the floor and collided with Cleo Rosa. A wall slid dizzyingly towards him and cracked his head. Through a swirl of pain, he thought: 'We're rotating! Fast! How? Why?' No answers came, just a single searing word: 'meteorite!' But he dismissed it at once. It couldn't be a meteorite. There were no alarms shrieking.

And suddenly he knew what it was.

The wild swift rotation continued for two minutes, then ceased. No-grav returned. On-surface blasts compensated for the erratic couple of minutes and brought no-spin again to Theeo; tranquillity, stability, the static normality of a planetoid without rotation.

Cleo Rosa's body twisted slowly and Gormal studied her injuries: cuts, bruises, nothing worse. He surprised himself by offering a fervent prayer. Eventually she regained consciousness and turned wide questioning eyes on him. 'Meteorite?'

'No, Sombre Blossom. One big enough to knock us so badly atwirl would have come inside. In addition, no alarms. So, no meteorite.' Her eyes appealed and he said tersely, 'Sabotage.'

'Again? But how?'

'Simple. A command to the computers controlling blasts; a command to blast hard for a while, to twirl us silly. Machines might berserk on us, yes? Therefore isn't it a wise precaution to give the power of override to super/inferior brains of flesh, like ours?'

'I see. More specifically, to B-blockers and above. It's sensible, yes.'

Gormal laughed, not altogether pleasantly. 'Sensible, I agree. Yet not on the part of the saboteur who, by displaying an authority reserved solely for just fifteen Thinkers and the Director, narrows the possibles to sixteen. A major mistake, I think.' Again the disturbing laugh sounded. 'A fair plan,' mused Gormal, 'which may be the undoing of someone. To utilise a brilliant dumb-brute machine; to take advantage of its compulsion to obey sixteen pre-fed voice patterns; to order a short vicious blast, then correction – yes, indubitably a fair plan. But fair is far from foolproof! You err, my enemy, you err!'

'He's made a slip-up, then?' asked Cleo Rosa.

'Or she. Or it, if we remember the Tuahi neuter in B! A shame the override-susceptible mechanisms don't record the identity of the overrider! Still, we can check who was where and when. Think-schedules, our memories, things like that. Prune sixteen possibles to . . . '

'Sixteen,' Cleo Rosa interrupted, with a mischievous smile. 'Don't forget time-devices on explosives. Even a blast-command with a prior command to delay. You could have done it yourself and got back here, with an alibi, long before the crunch.'

'Oh, I concede it! Further, I'd be inclined to select an alien as my prime suspect. A non-human. I can't envisage His Supreme Magnificence paying a human agent. Although I hear he's a devious object, and he might not pay at all.'

'What I don't understand . . . '

'Nor do I.' Gormal noticed her blank look and explained hurriedly. 'No, not telepathy. Just plain straightforward sympathy. Kindred feelings, identical doubts; no inter-species mental gulf, you see? Not at the moment, anyway.' He took both her hands, engulfing them in one of his own. 'Pardon the smell, but I don't understand one aspect of the affair, either: the minor acts of sabotage. Theft, yes; I comprehend it. But to attempt the hijacking of an organism, and meanwhile send it annoyances no more crippling than an insect on the eyeball, where's the consistency?'

'There doesn't seem to be any, Gormal. Twelve of us killed in the grappler incident.' She blushed, recalling her misplaced abuse of Gormal and the awkward apologies afterwards. 'And virtually simultaneously, these comparatively trivial things. Perhaps a few broken bones today, perhaps just superficial injuries. Nothing terrible, surely. So where's the point of it all?'

'Again, Lovely Nightshade, there doesn't seem to be any. That is, none that we can see. Yet remember lesson one: different races are different. Thought differs. Ambitions differ, as do their methods of execution. The idea of right and wrong varies. Therefore how do we locate the point if we can't understand the brain that plans?'

'Come in,' Pertra called, and Derek came in. 'Now, Dizzy, I've sent for you because I want you.'

'Sounds reasonable.'

'Lords of Void,' thought the Director, 'he's so unpredictable.' Pertra asked Derek to sit down. His voice was firm and his hand gestured to a chair on the other side of the desk. Since he'd been told to sit down, Dizzy went up. He hooked his feet in handholds and formed himself into an oblique protuberance on the ceiling, inverted. Pertra sighed. 'Very well. Just make yourself comfortable.'

'I have done, thanks.' Derek nodded to Arkon Vitch and wondered what his presence meant. 'You wanted me. I'm here.'

'Yes. We're going to talk. Our friend Arkon has brought me a strange tale. It concerns you.'

'They mostly do. Hi, Ark. The robot, is it?'

'Yes, Dizzy.' He sounded apologetic. 'I think it's for your own good.'

'So do I.' Pertra's neck was already aching from looking up. 'A disabled robot hardly counts, except when it's been shot. And then, not because of trivial damage but because a bullet implies a gun. Someone fired a gun and a robot was hit. This suggests three theories to me. First, a joke; irresponsible but possible. Second, more sabotage; very minor but probable. Three, an accident, a mischance, in so far as the robot wasn't intended as the victim. You were.' He held Derek with his eyes. 'What do you say to that?'

'Three sixes are twelve.'

Pertra began, 'I . . .' and stopped, determined not to lose his temper.

'In other words,' Derek elucidated, 'rubbish! Three sixes aren't twelve.'

'I see.' ('At least,' thought Pertra, 'I think I do.') 'You deny the third possibility?' Derek offered an upside-down affirmative and the Director sighed again. 'I expected you to. Though, with due apologies, I find in myself the effrontery to call you a liar.' Derek shrugged indifference. 'In fact, I'd stake my . . . ah . . . insecure position upon it. You're a liar.'

'I'm a liar, yes.'

Annoyance grew in Pertra's mind. Not speaking, he asked himself, 'Is this man to be suffered? I martyr myself! To strangle him and toss him into endless night would save much strain on my nerves!' But he knew it was the wrong approach and forced himself to speak gently. 'Dizzy, we are solicitous for your well-being. Arkon and I both noticed a certain apprehension in you recently. Follow this by what may have been an effort to shoot you . . .'

'Who do you think is after me?' Derek interrupted. 'And why?'

'So you admit . . . ?'

'No. Just for the sake of argument.'

'I couldn't even begin to guess who. As for the why – an old grudge, maybe; some person you've upset by your idio . . .' Pertra broke off and changed the word: 'Idiosyncrasies. Perhaps a very tiny wrong, real or imagined, has grown in a certain mind to unwholesome proportions and become an apparent motive for murder. I believe that's highly probable, taking into account an amazing though credible idea Arkon imparted to me. Please repeat it, Arkon.'

Cautiously, Vitch recited Vitch's Corollary, watching Derek for a reaction which didn't come. He'd told it Pertra merely as a time-filler and hadn't expected him to take much notice. Feeling uneasy, he thought: 'That could have triggered him off. One day he's going to explode and there'll be lots of pieces flying!' But Derek didn't react and Vitch was glad of it.

'An interesting idea,' Pertra resumed. 'Don't you think?'

'Sometimes.' Derek's eyelids drew down slowly, upwards, in a long lazy blink.

Irritation surged through Pertra as an involuntary clenching of the fists. Derek was obviously in one of his impossible moods. There'd be no sense issuing from his slack lips yet a while. Again the Director communed with himself subvocally: 'I'm positive he's in danger, but how can he be helped if he stays locked inside himself?'

'Listen, Dizzy,' he said quietly, 'we can't keep an eye on you all the time, which is clearly desirable if my suspicions are correct. Yet if you persist in playing a lone hand . . . '

'That's the way I like it. The way I am.'

'I know that!' Impatience had crept into Pertra's voice. 'And it's perilously wrong! You have to sleep. You don't have 360° vision. Against at least a hundred creatures in Thoughtworld you wouldn't stand a chance in a life-or-death fight . . . ' Unseen, Vitch shook his head in a silent denial. ' . . . so bearing all these things in mind, how can you hope to prevail? Assuming I'm right, that is?'

'It is, isn't it? Quite a sizeable assumption, too.'

'Demons of the Empire, Dizzy, you're not a fool!' Pertra blazed, with a sudden loss of control. 'I'm trying to help you, can't you see? Trying to save your life. Assuming I'm right.'

'You are.'

'And assume further that . . . ' He stopped. He went back six words. 'I'm *right*?' The voice was incredulous now, not at the truth, but at Derek's utterly unexpected admission. Surprisingly, Pertra found himself laughing. 'Dizzy, I'd rather bet my life on guessing the weight of the universe than on guessing which way you'll turn next!' The laughter ceased. 'However, to return to the problem . . . '

'Forget it. It'll resolve itself. You know what's under the plaque?'

It seemed an inconsequential question, but Pertra answered it. 'Unless you're intimating something I couldn't possibly fathom, tons of dirt and eleven dead men.'

'Right again. Eleven corpses in Thoughtworld, if we overlook the victims of the atrocity at the service. Eleven corpses. Only soon it'll be eleven plus one. That's twelve.'

'Meaning?'

'Meaning either somebody'll catch me or I'll get suspicious of somebody. And once I'm sure of 'em, they're dead!'

'That's murder, Dizzy. Taking the law into your own hands.'

'When it's me that's threatened,' Derek said solemnly, staring at his hands, 'that's exactly where it belongs!'

Chapter Eight

It was a small paragraph, heavily ringed in red ink: 'OBITUARY: On 14-4-245, at exactly six and seven-tenths hours after dawn, the death occurred under violent circumstances of Joab Lundren, then Prime Minister of New Athens. His passing is mourned by many and welcomed by many, and it may seem gruesomely coincidental that his murder transpired exactly six and seven-tenths years after The Day in 238. It is, however, no coincidence. *Requiescat in pace*. Perhaps. In the name of the Merrin Triad, Amen!'

Furiously, Lundren slammed the newspaper on to his desk. 'They're sick,' he thought, 'without compassion. Warped facetious vermin!' He glanced at the calendar-clock: 12-4-245, mid-morning. That gave him just over two days before they struck. And he knew they'd strike. They'd strike precisely when they'd predicted they would, violently. He wondered how. Another grenade? A suicidal fanatic coming right into the building? He didn't doubt they were capable of infiltrating so far; the memorial stone was fresh in his memory, as fresh as the painted letters on the wall. A bomb to blast the entire government complex?

He realised they were perfectionists. They paid fine attention to detail. A quick calculation verified their arithmetic; six and seven-tenths years since what they called The Day, 14-7-238. With twisted logic, they'd time their attack for six and seven-tenths hours after dawn, six and seven-tenths years after The Day. And they might be successful!

Sudden ice ran through him. Death, the old enemy, the feared – and here it was, in print, forecast to the minute. From the front sheet of the newspaper its title shrieked in brazen perverted humour: Mole's Digest – The Underground News. 'God,' thought Lundren, 'who could laugh at that? It's so foolish!' But he knew plenty of people did find it amusing, as they also chuckled at the light-hearted interpretation of the initial letters MOLE: the Merrin Organisation for Lundren's Extermination, as they'd also chuckle at his death! He thought irritably: 'They're playing with me. They'd already demonstrated that they could get into the courtyard, yet last night they'd been content merely to fling a handful of their pamphlets over the wall.' He pictured the rebels smugly tittering, happy in the knowledge of his knowledge of their powers.

A bell rang urgently on the intercom. 'What now?' he asked himself angrily, snatching up the receiver. He could hear voices chattering loudly at the other end, dozens of them, speculative. Ghost-fingers of premonition brushed the back of his neck. 'What is it this time?'

'The Confed, sir!'

The ghost-fingers started to stab with long, long-dead nails. 'The . . . Confed?' He cursed his startled pause, a sign of weakness, indecision, inability to meet a shock unruffled. The Confed? Were they coming to New Athens? 'Go on,' he ordered, controlled again.

'Theeo, sir!'

'Theeo?' He repeated it automatically, with a repeat of the chill nastiness slithering over and into his neck. 'The Confed? Theeo? Why can't the bastard be more coherent and specific?' His fingers tightened on the receiver. Other fingers tightened on his neck. 'Look, what is this? A bloody guessing-game?'

'No, sir, I mean, of course not, sir! No! Only we've picked them up on the scanners – Confed ships – the greater part of Squadron 17, massed around Theeo!' The voice waited for instructions.

The greater part of 17, massed around Theeo? Better there than converging on New Athens, anyway! Still, what were they doing up there? A tiny shower of relief assuaged Lundren's sweating brow, a cool dampness, a fact among a score of questions. It couldn't have anything to do with the

EA, or 17 would be dropping towards Peace Planet with no stopovers on the way. The secret was safe, so far.

'Any orders, sir?'

'Yes,' Lundren replied immediately, wondering what the orders would be. He was angling for time, determined not to show indecision. But so many things were coming all at once, so many dangers and problems! He made up his mind. 'Get me in touch with Theeo's Director, that new fellow Pertaara, or whatever his infernal name is!'

'Right away, sir!'

'I'm telling you, Sil, he's primed to go bang at absolutely any moment!' Arkon Vitch stated it flatly, then added significantly, 'With or without provocation as we'd understand it.'

The mask slurred Silver's speech. 'Pertra said we're all bombs. Just waiting for a flame or a plunger.'

'True.' He stared at her unreachable face, her lips a few feet away, a lifetime distant. 'And Dizzy's the biggest bomb I've met. There's enough explosive in him to destroy a world: memories, emotions, a whole lot of hate. Nothing you can define, but it's all there, waiting, but what, for him, makes a flame or a plunger?'

Silvery cheeks shone, jewelled eyes aflash with an effort at humour. 'We'll find out, Ark. When it's flamed or plunged.'

'Which will be too late!'

'You look scared, Ark,' she said softly, her hand in his.

'I am, and that's a fact! Scared of what he'll do when he blows. And who he'll do it to. Also . . . ' He paused, weighed his pride, then discarded it. He felt braver for the touch of her hand, brave enough to confess, 'I'm also scared of him personally. Oh, I know I'm no hero, but I've never admitted fear of another human before! What makes it worse is, I actually like the poor idiot. When he's rational, at any rate.'

Self-consciously, he related the incident of his slap to quieten Dizzy's hysteria, and the lightning return punch. 'Nobody's ever got one in against me as fast and hard as that. I appreciate he's second-to-none in no-grav; that gave him an advantage. But I'd swear he'd have managed it even if his hands had been tied.'

'His troubles have really got inside you, haven't they?'

'Inside me?' He released her hand to press a button. They passed through a door, walking slowly. 'Yes, they've got inside me. Although what worries me most is the effect they're having inside him! Pushing to burst out. I'd rather you were on the other side of the Confed when they do.' He smiled wryly. 'I'd rather I was, too!'

Another button depressed and they were in Communications. He checked panels beneath the visiplate; no record of any calls, no requests for anyone to call back, no numbers listed. Vitch's Corollary buzzed in his mind. Already he'd been widely congratulated on it; apparently Pertra had made a full-scale production about broadcasting the idea, and set it flowing like excited sap down every branch of the grape-vine he could discover.

He styled it the first cerebral breakthrough since his arrival; an epoch; a thought so obvious that no one ever thought of it before, perhaps not even Tynar himself. According to Pertra, it was marvellous. In Arkon's opinion, it was simply an idle thought over which the Director was making far too much fuss and behaving out of character. Moreover, the promulgation of Vitch's Corollary aroused a very real fear in the brain of its creator: that Dizzy Derek might in one of his lucid spells realise what had prompted the Corollary, then manifest displeasure at it in some un-predictable manner. 'Anyhow,' mused Arkon, 'there's a greater Breakthrough imminent. Maybe.'

'He's like Peace Planet, isn't he?' Silver's question took him off balance. He blinked and she explained. 'Dizzy, I mean. Too much suppressed for too long.'

'Hmmm, concisely put.' Sudden ardour came into Arkon's tone. 'Silver, he's in grave danger. Derek. Including the x-factor, only five of us know, so keep your lips tight and . . . ' He had to pull up, to swallow a bitterness of his own. His eyes avoided the mask. 'Someone sent a bullet after him. It may have happened before. Remember how edgy he was when we spoke to him after he'd gone crazy about someone's blocking Lundren? An imbecile the lad might be, but I'll stand by him! How many people do you suppose possess guns in Thoughtworld?'

She laughed at the action-mood in his eyes. 'Don't be silly, Ark! That way, you'll narrow the suspects down to probably a couple of hundred. Why, I own a gun myself!' He glanced a question. She spoke an answer. 'I used to travel a lot before I qualified for this place. Civilisation isn't civilised; I'm considered quite attractive. You never know . . .'.

'Yes, that makes sense. Obviously it's me that doesn't. Still, you're safe without it here. I suggest you give it Dizzy.' Privately, Arkon thought: 'Or is that just handing him the means of murder? Yes, but he has to defend himself, within the law or not. For which I'm certain he's more than adequately equipped even with no weapon other than himself!' Then aloud: 'How about it, Sil?'

'I'm not sure.' She hesitated, then found decision. 'Fair enough, I'll give it him. But I don't imagine he'll have the vaguest notion how to use it!'

'Probably not, but you can explain which end is which. He should assimilate the data nicely inside an hour. If he's on your wavelength at the time.'

'Is he ever?'

They laughed and a light flashed a summons. The visiplate warmed from blankness to an image: a young face, a neat suit. 'Theeo?' The normal/abnormal acknowledgement was conceded by Arkon. The face smiled. 'Thank you. Person-to-person from Prime Minister Lundren, Attica, New Athens. Would you mind fetching your Director?' The eyes lowered, as if checking a name. 'Oh, yes. Sciri Pertra, if you please!'

In his office, Pertra thought: 'It'd be wiser if they'd sent a human instead of you.' But diplomatically he kept his opinion quiet. There was nothing wrong with the Confed official. Pertra simply didn't consider him the best choice. 'Don't judge on externals,' he commanded himself.

Strapped into a chair, the official looked an habitually sad type: a sallow, slightly porcine individual, drably dressed. His close-set eyes were dull with the disillusioning experience of several hundred worlds. He extended a double-thumbed hand and said plaintively, 'Erranlal. Conf . . .'

'Erranlal? Ah yes, the similarity had suggested itself!'

'That's not unusual.' Erranlal glanced at the 2D of his brother Tynar, identical except for the eyes. 'In the family we gave him the puberty-name of Mirror Brain. He stared inside himself so much his introspection showed on the outside. Reflected. Not that his cerebration itself showed, only the fact of its presence. Even he couldn't understand what he was thinking about half the time!'

'Then you're here not only on behalf of the Confed but also because you're Tynar's brother?'

'No, that's pure coincidence. I'm glad of it though; nice to see what the family achieved. Part of it, that is. Me, I'm Slow Persistence.' He allowed himself a lip-twitch, a quarter-smile. 'I get results, but it takes longer. Parsecs of travel, loads of arduous headwork, rather than the intuitive short-cuts of the More Renowned One.'

'I see.' Pertra wondered if he'd been hasty in assuming a non-human to be the wrong choice. With all the indicators pointing at Benlhaut, perhaps a human would have been the wrong choice. He'd almost certainly concentrate on aliens, but if he were a xenophobe he might pick out the first that happened along, just for spite. Another non-human ought to act more warily, consider even humans as suspects, be more careful not to jump vindictively on a random victim – unless he too were a xenophobe! Erranlal, with his family interest, could be ideal. He'd do the job properly, for the sake of his brother's exalted memory. And with a name like Slow Persistence, he'd definitely be as positive as possible before passing judgement.

'Though if he's as slow as all that,' thought Pertra, 'we might be out in the wretched Empire before he passes judge-ment on Saril!' With peace of mind in mind, Pertra shied away from the thought. 'He seems dependable, so let's de-pend on him.' The Director knew he could forget the Thir-teen for the moment. They'd less distance to cover and more reason to cover it: therefore they'd be way behind the Confed. That was the fashion in which they did things, stupidly and sluggishly.

'Confed Plenipotentiary,' said the Tuahi, prodding himself. 'I don't use the title much; just scare folks with it now and then, when I have to. I'm just an ordinary troubleshooter. Trouble is, making trouble lie still long enough so you can shoot it. A problem, that!' He touched a thick folder he'd clipped to the desk. 'So's that! Your problem. Now mine, of course. I've scanned the contents: a hundred-word problem, condensed to about ten-thousand.' Again his lips twitched. 'I'd prefer the story as you tell it.'

Pertra told him Theeo's story: sabotage, tractor beams, sabotage and grapplers. And an endangered Dizzy Derek.

Erranlal's ingrained frown deepened. 'Oh? I hadn't heard that. Shot at? Curious! Maybe separate, maybe connected. We'll see. Anything abnormal about him?'

'Anything *ab*normal? Void-Lords, you haven't met him! He eats, visits the lavatory, talks when he feels like it. Thinks a bit – correction, thinks a lot! Doesn't reflect much on him externally. He does his work well. Sleeps. Probably dreams. That far, he's normal. Otherwise . . . ' Pertra let silence speak for a while. 'You'll see.'

'It sounds as if he's an oddity. They mostly mean difficulties. Such as . . . '

'Excuse me,' Pertra said into the door-buzz. 'Please enter!'

Vitch did. 'Pardon me, Sciri, but you're wanted. Visiplate. Lundren.'

'Indeed? What might he be chasing?' Termination already? It didn't worry the Director. 'Apologies, friend Erranlal; it seems one above me down on New Athens requires me. I must leave you for some minutes. Or you wish to accompany me?'

'For Lundren? Not worth the effort, thanks!' Erranlal spoke disparagingly and Pertra wondered why. He didn't expect an answer to the question he hadn't asked, but he got one. 'I have a surprise for a certain person high in a certain government. There are rumours. Nothing definite, just whispers. They hint at a secret organisation on Peace Planet. Not the ideological offspring of Lev Merrin, either. More sinister. I have to look into the matter. By the proxy of a dozen ships under hand-picked commanders, tomorrow I shall do so. But,' a finger touched down-curling lips as a caution, 'not a word of this. Nor of me. I can rely on you?'

'Absolutely. I wouldn't tell him his name if he forgot it.' Pertra risked a smile, but thought: 'There! I'm on record with the Confed as not being pro-Lundren. So what? There's no law against it. Up here.' He had every confidence the Confed Plenipot shared his feelings. A couple of quiet seconds and the smile was returned, Erranlal's most energetic lip-twitch yet.

'He's not likely to forget it,' replied the official. 'He lives by it.'

'Well put,' mused Pertra, and put himself outside his office, following Vitch. He wasn't surprised to see Silver in Communications; he'd learned to expect her in the immediate neighbourhood of Vitch during out-of-Think hours. What did surprise him was the image in the plate: a young face, a neat suit. The young face glanced down, then glanced up. 'Director Pertra?'

'No other! I match my 2D?' A trace of anger couldn't be kept out of his tone. 'You're suspicious? You suspect imposters?'

Arrogant eyes stared, then finally lowered before Pertra's. 'I'll connect you . . . ' the eyes flickered defiance, ' . . . sir!'

It took longer than was necessary. Pertra guessed this was a deliberate part of Lundren's policy: make them wait, get them edgy, don't talk to them as equals. The policy suited the personality, in Pertra's view. It stank.

Lundren appeared, falsely jovial. 'Hello, Professor Pertra, I hope I find you well?'

The Director was too perceptive to be fooled by a genial mask with hard eyes. Plainly Lundren wanted something. Pertra didn't intend to help him ask. He waited.

'A friendly call, Professor. Settling in all right?' He received no answer but swept on regardless. 'Good. A happy worker is an efficient one.' The public smile shone, all teeth. 'Oh, by the way, I knew there was something else . . . '

'Here it comes,' thought Pertra, pursing his lips, determined not to say much.

'The Confed. I notice Squadron 17's pretty thickly clustered around Theeo. My Meteorological Department happened to see them; routine scan, of course. Probably mistook them for high-flying clouds.' Lundren laughed. It sounded like an arctic gale pretending to be a summer breeze. 'Nothing wrong up there, is there?'

'No, not really,' Pertra said guardedly. 'Little touches of annoying sabotage, lately. Another attempt at theft. I've notified the Thirteen officially, but in view of the larger issue I decided to contact the Confed direct.' In silence he watched tight lips tighten.

'*You* decided . . . ? Yes, yes, quite correct.' Visibly, an inner battle raged; it shifted face-lines. 'Well, at least you'll be safe with such a military multitude round you.' A hoarse noise rattled in Lundren's throat and emerged, masquerading as a chuckle.

'Indeed.' Pertra didn't need to force a smile. The words he wouldn't let himself say amused him: 'We'll be okay, yes. Only tomorrow, Adamantine Employer, part of the multitude peels off for New Athens. If you're hiding anything, you'd best get ready to hide yourself. Deep.'

'I'll leave it with you, then, Pertra.' Anxiety clamoured raucously in Lundren. Did the Confed have any ulterior motive in being so close to New Athens? Was another rebellion planned, to follow the projected murder in two days? He mastered the internal uproar. 'That's all, I think.'

'Sure there's nothing else?' Pertra asked ingenuously, smiling inside.

'No, nothing more. That's all for now.' Without a thank you, Lundren blanked. Without sympathy, Pertra realised he'd been talking to a very worried man.

The interruption irritated Derek. It was one thing to be sidetracked from Think by the wanderings of his own mind, momentarily ripped out of contemplation by cerebral digressions: thoughts of the enormity of the hoped-for Breakthrough tickling his brain despite the near-ideal conditions in Theeo. Such mental meanderings were tolerable. What he didn't like were unauthorised and physical interruptions.

He didn't like people clumping into his room, disturbing Think.

He heard the door open, and turned to see who to be angry at. But anger suffocated under amazement when he thought he saw Tynar. Tynar was dead, so by rights he shouldn't be walking anywhere, least of all into a Thinker's chamber when it was engaged. Probably Tynar's shade, he concluded. Beneath Derek's gaze filed a glum procession: a glum Erranlal and several glum attendants in uniform. Erranlal introduced himself, stating his business. 'Your Director told me to familiarise myself with the place. Get the feel of it. It feels awkward.'

'What did the outside sign say?' Dizzy demanded inconsequentially.

Erranlal reflected before reciting. ' "In Think". In capitals.'

'Exactly! "In Think",' Dizzy echoed. 'That means *I'm* in here, in Think. And *you* stay out there until the sign goes out. Then you come in.' He astonished the other by standing on his head, way above Erranlal's. 'So out you go while the sign's on. Then later, in you come while the sign's off. Bye-bye.'

Comprehension dawned. 'You wouldn't be Derek, would you?'

'I would if that were my name. And since it is, I am.'

'I guessed as much.' Tynar's brother realised Pertra certainly hadn't understated Derek's abnormality. 'Sorry about the infringement. We'll get the feel of the place elsewhere.' Suddenly his tone hardened. 'But we've a serious job to do, remember! Cooperation would help. Non-cooperation might be construed as standing in the way of a Confed Plenipotentiary.'

It was intended to intimidate and it might have worked with an ordinary person. It didn't with Derek. 'Standing in your way? You're on the stripwalk; I'm in the air. I'm not impeding you. Out!'

Erranlal got out, with a poor opinion of Derek. The retinue followed. 'Here ends tranquillity,' ruminated Derek, imagining Thoughtworld crawling with Confed agents. They'd be checking all the sabotage sites, snooping, interviewing and generally getting underfoot. He decided to remain airborne as much as possible, so they'd be farther underfoot and therefore not underfoot so much. Then he thought: 'Tranquillity? Christ!' and remembered the lack of it; grapplers, deaths, explosions and strangling cords. He backpedalled mentally and amended the idea. It wouldn't be the end of calm; it would be an aggravation of existing non-calm.

He didn't envy the Confed their task, but he considered it could be made easier. Still, Erranlal must have brains enough to sort it out for himself. With regard to the computerised wobble-strike, there could only be sixteen people to choose from: the overriders, fifteen Thinkers and Pertra. In his search for the perpetrator of that particular incident, Erranlal needn't go lower than B-block.

'Thanks, Silver,' Dizzy muttered, feeling more confident on his own account as he thought of the gun she'd given him. His confidence soared to a sense of invincibility, then plunged down as he remembered where the gun was: in the cupboard in his quarters, out of reach. He couldn't bring himself to carry it. The touch of cold lethal metal made something cold twist painfully inside him. It triggered off a memory and knotted his mind. It flicked into him the poignant recollection of a dead girl:

'Arms of marble, eyes of sapphire,
'Death-glaze filming over . . . '

Crying, Derek thought of a small, locked-up, handwritten book. Sobbing, he recalled the words inside it. He pictured her dead face. Spherical tear droplets drifted on air, moisture globes containing terrible sorrow.

Chapter Nine

The Thirteen! The thought drew Pertra's eyes to the date-panel: 13-4-245. Today Lundren might develop a bad headache without physical pain. A dozen specially selected ships, with orders from Erranlal, had left the vicinity of Theeo. Soon, they'd be on New Athens. If Lundren had anything whose discovery he feared, Erranlal's subordinates wouldn't be long in uprooting it. The Director made a wish: 'Best of luck to them. I hope they do unearth something.' Knowing Lundren, it was more than possible.

Troubles trickled in Pertra's mind, with attendant questions. The tractor beam and grappler assaults, did they originate where they seemed to, namely in the Empire? The sabotage was so undramatic it was scarcely more than adult vandalism, but why such pettiness, why not totally disabling acts? The bullet that had failed to catch up with Dizzy Derek – in whose plans did Derek's death figure? For some reason, the last question disturbed him more than the others; the least of Theeo's problems, yet it nagged him the most. Why? Perhaps because he was fond of Dizzy. He didn't want him to come to any harm. But indubitably somebody did. Who? Had Dizzy offended someone, even hurt someone in his unrevealed past? Surely not! He was just a crazy man with a crazy name.

'Ah, that name!' Pertra's hand slapped the desk as he got at the foundation of his preoccupation with Derek: that crazy name. Dizzy? It was stupid. Who would call a child Dizzy? Either his parents were fools or . . . On impulse, Pertra left his desk and opened a filing-cabinet. He took out Dizzy's folder, suppressing a shiver of strange uncomfortable prescience. Unsteadily he fluttered papers and located a name, then stared. Derek's name actually *was* Derek – his first name, anyway. And his second . . . ?

Merrin! There it was, unmistakable: Derek Merrin, birthplace New Athens. 'Ah, I begin to see!' breathed Pertra. He remembered what Dizzy had insisted were his parents' names: Bob and Rhoda. It was almost certainly true. 'Bob Merrin. Bob Merrin.' Pertra repeated it until the association clicked. The trinity of revolutionary leaders killed in 238: Lev Merrin, Karl Merrin, Robert Merrin; young Lev at the top, aided by his father Karl and his uncle Robert. 'Yes, yes, much is explained! Extinct Lev, I salute your remarkable cousin, that mystery we know as Dizzy Derek!'

This time the nightmare was worse. This time the nightmare was the regular one, the recurrent sleep-haunter of the past seven years. If a month went by without it torturing him at least ten times, Derek counted himself fortunate. He knew that if it got any more horrible, if it came any more frequently, they'd find him some morning as empty of life as *she'd* been. They'd discover a corpse swinging in its webbing, swinging still in no-grav from its final futile threshing against the shadows in the shadow-land of awful dreams. A Derek no longer Dizzy, a Derek no longer really Derek, a shrunken flesh-lump which had lost its slender hold on sanity and its no-more-secure grip on life. Very dead! As she was! As she'd already been when he'd found her!

Frantically, Derek swam through the black dragging waters of a terrible sleep. Desperately, he fought to surface from a sleep-sea that sought to drown him in nightmare. His screams frozen silent in a parched throat, he lashed the clinging murk and scrambled clear of the suffocating waves, awake. Cold sweat drenched him. Horror lay like an anaesthetic on his mind, numbed his body and his powers of thought. After twenty minutes in a dark borderland, he realised he could move.

'I'm not dead!' It was always his first rational thought, often thought with irrational regret. Sometimes it seemed peaceful death would be preferable to the living torment of nightmares about death and violence and *her*! In clumsy near-panic, he fumbled out of the cocoon. He trod space for an apparent eternity as he settled to the floor. Mag-boots on, he felt better – incomprehensibly, since he hated to wear them. He decided it must be because they maintained the illusion of stability. While the boots held him down, fear couldn't whirl him up and away in a vortex which could only take him to the gates of death and beyond.

He clicked the light on and drowned willingly in a floor of bright illumination. Shadows leapt in the room, but the shadows in his mind receded, dying. For the moment, he could tolerate being alive. Remembering the *real* nightmare, he compared it with the one he'd suffered after the first attempt on his life. An unsuccessful attempt had led to an awful dream. A successful attempt – her strangulation, different yet indisputably no failure – led him time and again into a more awful dream.

There was only one way to exorcise her ghost temporarily: embrace it, admit its presence and its existence, reach out for it, cling to it and swear dreadful vengeance on its behalf, on her behalf. Then, for a while, it would vanish. She would vanish, until next time. So he spoke to her: 'You'll sleep well inside my head when vengeance is accomplished. Therefore I'll sleep well, too. And vengeance will be accomplished. I swear it!' Aloud, he committed himself to a death for a death. 'We'll both sleep well someday!' He wondered when. Would it be the slumber of grim satisfaction or the eternal rest of death? But how could death be eternal rest? She was dead, yet she definitely wasn't resting! She lived on in his head, too undeniable to be imaginary. She was reality. She wandered perpetually along the gloomy corridors of his brain, a night-flitting movement that would be stilled by nothing but another murder to avenge hers.

Derek did what he had to do. He unlocked a drawer, withdrew the one possession which really meant anything to him apart from his hate. It kept his hate at fever-pitch, gave him a purpose in life. Once the purpose had been fulfilled, he could sleep unhaunted and remember her as she must have been in life, vibrant and beautiful. Meanwhile, her shade, appeased, could go . . . where? He didn't know, but he was sure the ghost would benefit.

Sitting down, he laid on his knees a small diary and strapped himself to the chair. Then he read a neat evocative entry: 'This has been the most hideous day of my life. I've never seen such atrocities, even in larger wars than this. Though perhaps it doesn't class as a proper war, just a civil disturbance that's disturbed a whole planet – and me! The rebels say they're fighting for freedom; the other New Athenians say they're free already. Who knows the truth of it? All I know is, it's a shame people can't behave sensibly. The locals can curse us all they want: "Interfering busy-bodies! We didn't ask you to come!" "Go home, you old bitch!" Old? Me? At eighteen? But without the Confed Mobile Medical Arm, unasked or not, they'd be in a bigger mess than they are. And God, they *are* in a mess! When I've written this – as a lesson for my grandchildren, maybe – I'll sleep like the hundreds of dead I've seen today. I saw the "loyals" catch the insurgents' leader, Merrin, and literally tear him to pieces.'

Derek's hand tightened on the little book. Lev! The name screamed in his mind, another reason for murder. He read on: 'He was a very handsome man and I just can't believe he was the power-crazy maniac Lundren makes him out to be. Perhaps he was misguided, at most. So were thousands of others all over the world. To rise up like that, simultaneously, in every major city took planning and courage, or something. I know they'd got offworld arms; I know the "loyals" had only tools and knives and things. But it simply can't be true that the system's perfect and all the rebels are insane.' 'It isn't,' Derek said with feeling. 'Far from it.' Then he continued to read from the diary: 'They'd been screened, hadn't they? How about re-screening the animals I saw rip Merrin to bits? And killed babies for the fun of it? And stone poor Doctor Pol to death as he was helping the wounded? God! I can't bear to write any more!'

The entry was dated Day 14, Sevenmonth, 238. Derek had found her on the morning of Day 15, a once-lovely girl in a nurse's uniform. Her clothes bore the bloodstains of people she'd helped, perhaps saved. She'd been hanged from a lamp-post by a drunken mob. In memory, he could still hear their voices as they drifted into the distance: liquor-slurred yells, shouts of triumph at the end of the rebels.

'The end?' thought Derek. 'That was just a beginning! In time . . . ' But he couldn't follow through to the future. The past had hold of him too tightly: the rabble that had slaughtered the nurse – plus God knew how many other innocent doctors and well-intentioned young women – smashing everything in sight, destroying their own property as they set out on a wild rampage.

Attica had seen violence in those hectic days and so had many another city: unsteady Lundren supporters, noisily celebrating victory over an outnumbered foe; the same so-called conquerors, angrily turning against each other at a single wrong word; death and mutilation even after Lev's rebellion had been crushed; long-suppressed aggression bursting out, with Lev's anti-Lundren opinions touching flame to a powder-barrel which must soon have exploded anyway, on some pretext. Peace Planet? 'Hardly,' Derek told himself, gently closing the diary. 'They'd been sweet-talked by Lundren so much they believed it!'

Without a shred of sympathy, he could see their specious reasoning as they tore into Lev's tiny bands with a ferocity out of all proportion to the threat: 'We're citizens of Peace Planet. Therefore we're peaceful. Therefore this killing is right.' At any rate, it would run something like that. They'd been conditioned by Lundren, programmed to believe in the myth of Peace Planet. Probably most of the population still did, but a minority must even today cling to the aims and ideals of Lev Merrin, secretly plan insurrection and the overthrow of Joab Lundren, and the removal of a megalomaniac whose original intentions had been admirable but whose brain had twisted at some point in the time-path.

Derek was out of touch with the rebels these days. He wasn't active any more and wasn't part of the organisation. He operated alone – no, he merely *hoped* alone – motivated only by the lust for personal revenge. His thoughts crawled back to the girl, to the empty street, the lamp-post, the hanging body in a blood-splattered nurse's uniform. What could he use? He had to cut her down, but he couldn't reach. 'Why did I have to cut her down?' He still didn't know. Releasing her from the rope wouldn't release her from death.

He couldn't just sever the rope and simultaneously sever the bonds that tied her to a dimension beyond life. Nevertheless, he had to cut her down. She didn't deserve to twirl rope-held, a butt for the abuse and hatred of other mobs which might pass.

'If only I could give her a proper burial!' He spoke the words aloud now, strapped to the chair, as he'd spoken them aloud in the street. Memory slithered back to Attica. He looked up at her: soiled uniform, hair like a golden wind-rustled wheatfield. Death had transformed the beauty of her face into horror. Her blue eyes seemed about to erupt from her head. A limp foot brushed his cheek as she moved dead. A table! It lay discarded on its side against a house. The 'loyals' must have used and dragged her up on to it, kicking, struggling. Then they may have sent someone shinning up the post, to secure the rope and slip the noose around her pretty neck. They may have jumped down, laughed, and pulled the table away and . . .

Derek fetched the table, positioning it next to the post, beneath her. Her feet flopped along the polished surface. He climbed up and took a knife from his pocket. Marks on the blade testified to his part in the insurgence. There were visible scars on his body, and scars on his mind, invisible but more hurtful. Few people survived 238 unscathed. Thousands didn't survive at all. He put a strong arm around her slender waist. She was warm with sunglow, not life. He hugged her to him, to take the weight. In other circumstances, it would have been enjoyable. In these circumstances, it made him weep.

Still squeezing her in a passionate embrace, he slashed the rope. She came free. Her weight dropped, heavier than he'd expected. It snatched at his arm, streaking pain across his shoulder. He couldn't hold her! The table crashed over and they tumbled to the hard ground. It hurt Derek, although it couldn't hurt her. He hit the street first, finishing up on his back on the bottom, under her. Breath slammed out of his lungs and her soft breasts pushed at him, prodded down at him urgently with hideous prohibited sexuality.

Her body draped him, lay heavy on his, desirable but dead. Her arms snaked around his neck, moving as though

106

alive. She seemed to be returning his passionate hug. Not yet stiff, her fingers stroked his throat. They were so warm! They caressed him, fondled him, ran along his flesh and chilled him despite their warmth. Then in dreadful slow-motion, dream-like, her face settled firm, demanding, beautiful and awful on to his – a warm face, a dead face, a face with eyes that bulged blue. And she kissed him. Dead lips glued themselves to his. They pressed his mouth, stopped his scream and nearly stopped his heart. He wriggled in blind unthinking panic beneath a lovely body which was dead. He squirmed in red unthinking terror beneath full red lips which were dead. She kissed him with dead ardour. She was crushing him as he writhed. Her mouth pushed at his mouth – a corpse-kiss! It was then that his mind snapped.

Outside the door there was furtive movement. The work had to be done quietly and quickly. A tool-bag hung. Implements were extracted, used and put back. Once, a clumsily wielded screwdriver clattered against the wall of Derek's room. A heartbeat increased in sudden horror. Would it wake him? Would he hear? Silence. It wasn't a long job. It didn't require much mechanical knowledge. It was as easy as killing a fly. Fingers curled around the tool-bag and pulled it away down the corridor. Very shortly, Derek should be dead.

Most memories blurred in Dizzy's mind, but the memory of her wouldn't blur. It stayed large and close, a part of him. He wasn't sure he could live without it. Often he wasn't sure he could live with it. He returned the diary to its drawer, beside Silver's gun. The drawer closed, yet no drawer closed on memory. It remained open, vivid and clamorous. It hurt almost unbearably, but he had to bear it.

A glance at the cocoon and he wondered whether to get back into it. Would he be able to sleep now? He thought so, but there was no guarantee that the nightmare wouldn't come back. Even if he slept, the night still had ghosts with which to torment him. There was danger outside his skull and danger inside it. He asked himself which was the greater. No answer came.

A tear glistened in each eye, unashamed and unshed. A lump quivered in his throat and caught. Breath caught in his throat, too. He thought it must be reaction. It wasn't. The tears touched his cheeks. He felt dampness. The lump stayed in his throat. And he still couldn't breathe. He gulped for oxygen. There wasn't any.

Panicky hands slapped the straps free and fought the mag-boots off. Fire blazed in his chest. An inferno raged in each air-empty lung. It was similar to being strangled. The pain of it merged with the pain of memory. Physical and mental anguish tore at him. He hadn't breathed for twenty seconds. He might never breathe again. Because somebody had killed the fans! Incredulously, he stared at them all in turn. None of them were moving. An immobility like the immobility of death lay on them, but he had to get out.

'Some bastard means me!' he thought. 'Some bastard's been busy!' The odds against the fans stopping on their own were immense. Presumably somebody had also cut out the automatic alarm pulse which would have brought along a repair squad. Well, he'd just have to call the robots himself, later – if later existed for him. At the door, breathless, he cursed the hermetic sealing. Without it, oxygen could have leaked through from outside. Or was the corridor airless, too? Doubtful. Somebody had expected him to be tucked up snug in his cocoon and expire there in a cubic capsule of carbon-dioxide.

Somebody was going to have to be murdered. The door opened. Derek flopped out, clinging to a hold. Oxygen flooded in, great gasps of it. It tasted marvellous. It tasted of life itself. He thought: 'Third time unlucky, again.' His smile was a predatory leer, the precursor of someone's violent death. He didn't know whose death, but he had his suspicions and intuitions. He reminded himself that Tynar's Hypothesis had been a touch of intuition, later backed up by research into the early days of rocketry on a thousand worlds. If Tynar could follow up a guess, so could Derek. But it wouldn't culminate in the creation of a planet. It would culminate in the destruction of a person.

For the first time ever, he was thankful for the agonising memory. The dead girl had saved his life. If the nightmare hadn't awakened him when it did, he'd never have awoken again. He arranged a repair team, then spent hours sweeping through the air of Thoughtworld. He flew with a fantastic pleasure in life, thinking death. When the exercise had tired him, he set off at a leisurely pace and visited every block down as far as F. He stopped everyone he saw, watching for their reaction as he shouted, 'Look! I'm still alive!' Nobody reacted properly.

Chapter Ten

'You incompetent fool! Can't you do anything right?'
Lundren's voice was a roar. The report of a third failure
had outraged him. He couldn't tolerate the idea of a Merrin
still being alive. Nor was Derek merely *a* Merrin. A father-
son relationship linked him to one of the insurrection's two
seconds-in-command. Derek was Robert Merrin's son,
Karl's nephew, Lev's cousin; in all probability the nearest
kin of the Triad to have survived 238. Lundren took his
survival almost as a personal insult. 'I tell you, he's got to
be wiped out!' he shouted into the visiplate.

'I've tried, but . . . ' In Thoughtworld, in Communications,
speech froze.

'Don't I know it! Tried three times. Bungled it three times.
God, he's only human! He can be killed. So kill him!' 'Like
the decent citizens of Attica executed his criminal cousin,'
thought the Prime Minister. Lundren always viewed Lev
Merrin's death as a well-deserved execution. No court had
condemned him, but Lundren considered the mob had saved
a lot of legal fuss. He pondered on Merrin's career. Merrin
had been a promising young politician, until he went rene-
gade, left public service, quit the Thirteen and turned rebel.
Lundren could forgive him for the events of 238 more easily
than he could forgive him for what he'd done whilst employed in a responsible position by the Thirteen when he
had stubbornly and implacably opposed Lundren's efforts to
achieve Thinker status. Even now, Merrin was a barrier.
Even dead, he lived on as an influential name. His memory
kept ablaze a monstrous fire of resistance, a fire which, given
luck and skill, would in a few hours burn its chief enemy
into oblivion.

Lundren noted the message of the calendar clock: four and a half hours to live. It was a frightening message, a burden made heavier by the inability of a bungling fool in Theeo. Inwardly, Lundren swore. His stern unsmiling features glared from the plate, lips tightly compressed, eyes pale and unwavering – a frightening face, inspiring hatred as well as fear; a face that brought recollection of a barbed couplet it had evoked years ago.

I rate the man a hateful man. I urge you not to trust his
Adamantine face and his Rhadamantine justice.

'Only words,' thought the communicant, 'but not empty words!' You had to use words. How else could you attack the man? With conventional weapons? Yes, if you could get near him. Through the law? Not a chance, because for every legal gun you could swing at him, he could swing a hundred bigger ones. He could hide behind legal barriers, untouchable, invulnerable and mocking.

Which left words, and words, moulded skilfully, really *could* hurt him. Lundren proved it by his furious reaction to *JL: An Attack!*

He holds inside him, hot as fever, many an olden grudge;
Moves swiftly to forgive himself, leaps angrily to judge –
When judgement is against another, and can be thrust
                                                          home where
It maims a foe. 'Trade blow for blow!' he cries. 'Come –
                                                          if you dare!'

Yes, *that* had stung him! 'As it stung my pocket,' flashed the thought, 'stung it absolutely empty.' But money didn't count much. It had been worth it just to fashion loathing around prosody, to know several thousand copies had escaped the court's destruction order. Writing the verse – even paying financially for the crime of having written it – had been a pleasure to set against the pain of what followed.

As though from a distance not only of space, Lundren was still speaking. He received perfunctory affirmatives, nega-

111

tives, short answers, only partial attention. It was difficult to concentrate on both Lundren and the hatred, the memory, the resolve to finally break free of his influence and risk the consequences. One fraction of the brain made pretence of full attention. The remainder determined to throw off the fear-shackles, to atone for past wrongs by confession and exposure.

'Hell, I wish I'd never let him coerce me into this! I actually like Derek; I don't want to harm him. Thank God I failed! I've got to shake off that rock-faced bastard's stranglehold!' Yet always there lingered his threat – no, not merely a threat! Like Pertra's warning during the grappler assault, it had been much more than a threat. It had been a solemn promise.

' "Financial ruin last time, eh? Oh, I believe I can manage far worse things that that!" He'd actually laughed, a real happy laugh. "It would help me to have someone up in the heavens, where you came from." In the heavens? Why didn't I stay in the heavens? What diabolical fate made our paths cross? A vacation elsewhere, or a day later . . . "You understand, I hope? *Far* worse things! Imprisonment, perhaps? Five years? Ten, fifteen? *Life?*"

'What a futile protest I put up! "You've nothing on me now, so . . . " "Good Lord, do I need anything! I've an imagination. You've a past. Let's see . . . attempted murder, with a motive easily unearthed? Sounds nice."

'Murder? It does sound nice. If I could get at him. Did he let me get close that day? Did he search me out specially? Does it matter? "Believe me, I can make any charge stick. Whether with the glue of true guilt or with an artificial adhesive. I have contacts. And power." '

Then there followed reluctant acceptance and submission, because of pure fear. Lundren had acquired someone up in the heavens. And he'd added bitingly, 'You're not really cut out to be a Thinker, you know.'

'Which makes two of us! The other's staring at me right now.' Joab Lundren still glared from the visiplate, issuing orders.

Something floated from under a table. Lundren gaped. 'God!'

'No,' said Derek, 'it's only me. Hello, Cleo.'

She whirled, turning a furious face on him. Beauty blurred, buried beneath shock, terror and sudden hate. All recent thoughts of regret died, killed by the dread of being killed. Self-reproach melted into abomination. She trembled before a more immediate threat than Lundren's. Derek clung to the table, held down by it, airborne vengeance. His face was pale and expressionless, frightening in its utter lack of visible emotion. He nodded to Cleo Rosa. 'Weapon.' He glanced at Lundren. 'Finger on the trigger.'

She tensed, ready to spring in search of escape. 'What . . . ?'

'A lovely day to kill,' Dizzy finished, grinning.

'Isn't it?' Defiance showed itself as a flush of hot blood rushing to her cheeks. She knew she'd be forced to kill him now, if he didn't kill her first. The door seemed a million miles away.

'Cleo of Theeo. Disruptive flower.' An expression appeared: amusement, cold and hard. Then his features firmed into thoughtfulness. 'I should have guessed straight away, from the weapon. The strangling cord, Asia-Terra. A natural choice. Still . . .'

She dived head-first for the door, slapped the release. Then she was through and Derek was cursing his introspection. He waved gaily to the stupefied image of Lundren and dashed in pursuit. He hadn't trailed her here just to have his suspicions confirmed and then lose her. This had to be the last round, for one of them. As she flew from pursuing revenge, Cleo Rosa recalled Lundren's icy words: 'You're not really cut out to be a Thinker.' They'd seemed foolish at the time, but she knew he'd appraised her correctly. Perspicacity or a shot in the dark? It didn't matter. The weight of space crushed and oppressed her, and her hideous agoraphobia had worsened since she came to Theeo. Did that bear out Vitch's Corollary? Probably. Anyway, she definitely wasn't cut out to be a Thinker. Through bitterness at the net of circumstance in which fate's intrigue had enmeshed her, she thought dejectedly: 'I'm not cut out to be a murderess either!' But evidently she'd got to be one, or die.

Derek was gaining. There was no one about. He wondered

if it were fortunate or unfortunate and finally decided it was a good thing. Although a bypasser's intervention would possibly delay her, the absence of any bypassers kept it a private duel. 'Now,' he thought, 'make a grab and . . . ' He got a tight grip on her ankle with a flying tackle. The tug of his arm slowed her. They drifted together, a picture of apparent serenity. Hate seethed inside them both, like loathsome grubs gnawing beneath a bed of coloured peaceful flowers.

Derek tried to twist towards the floor, to drag her down. She was too supple and slippery in air. Somehow he had to get grounded. He didn't like boots, but he needed to struggle into a pair. If he could reach a walkway without letting go of her, then rely solely on his superior strength . . .

Her free foot smacked him hard in the mouth. Blackness smothered his brain long enough for her to shrug off his grip. She was loose in air. Teeth were loose in his gums. A shower of blood globules misted around him as he shook his head to clear it. It half-cleared. To his surprise, she didn't flee. She dropped and scrambled into boots. It looked like a mistake, but it wasn't. Derek hesitated, unsure. Should he land away from her and boot-up, then close in for a fight he couldn't lose? Or had she some devious plan, some reason for handing him the chance he wanted? Maybe as soon as he'd put on a pair of boots, she'd unboot and fly, gaining a few precious seconds. The question of where she could possibly go to find safety never occurred to him.

He decided to take the advantage she'd given him. Forget superior strength. Use his skills in no-grav while she was pinned down. It was too good an opportunity to miss. He swerved for her and dived down fast. Her hands came up to meet him and he grabbed them. Then suddenly she dipped her body slightly, turned his momentum against him, and he was hurtling across the room without the smallest hope of controlling his horizontal plunge. The wall hit him and again came the blackness.

When he climbed out of it there was pain: a throbbing in his head, shrieking streaks of agony in his shoulder. And another surprise: she was still in view. He could only have been out for an instant. He thought frantically: 'What now?'

114

Would she seize the chance to finish him. Derek realised she could do it. He hadn't fully recovered. The tiniest movement brought increased pain to his head. Even thinking seemed to hurt. One arm hung useless at his side. He knew he couldn't fight her off if she closed in for the last act. How would she do it? Had she a weapon? A little knife would be big enough. Crack his skull against the wall a couple of times and his feeble resistance would cease. Then she could continue cracking at her leisure until unconsciousness changed into something more permanent.

'Come on! Get it over if you're going to!' Panic surged in his stomach. Subjectively, time was crawling. He'd managed so many thoughts in such a short space. He tried to push off from the wall, but it was a weak effort and he barely moved. He just waited, watching.

Cleo Rosa arose from the boots. Indecision danced across her beautiful but frightened face. To kill or to run? The question was clear in her expression. She stared at Derek, appraised his position and shrugged. She couldn't assess how bad his injuries were. He could be feigning some of the distress. He could even be feigning all of it. To kill or to run?

She ran. Haste fluttered a flurry of poemed papers behind her and she ran. Personal fear conquered Lundren's commands and she ran. Her legs stamped down on nothing as she channelled the impetus of boot-release and vanished from the room. She left in a graceful fast-float, heading somewhere or anywhere or nowhere. She didn't know. For the moment, a hiding-place would suffice. She needed time to think.

Derek's gaze followed her as she went. Again he pushed at the wall, more successfully. He drifted, his mind awakening a little. With his good hand he snatched a hold, dragging himself forward. By degrees his speed increased and he took up the pursuit in pain. He knew he'd find her. It seemed wrong to kill a woman, somehow. And it seemed absolutely right to kill a would-be murderer. To allow her to live would be gallantry – and stupidity. To destroy her would be murder – and self-preservation. It didn't take him long to sort the problem out.

He knew he'd kill her.

He left the brief interlude of misplaced casuistry behind him and went after Cleo Rosa. Scattered raindrops of pity splashed on the fire of his determination, dampening his blazing resolve. An inner conflict raged. He had to squash it. He squashed it.

There could be no mercy, no handing her over to authority. This was a battle he had to win alone. He viewed it as being above the law. Or below it. At any rate, outside it. 'I am a law unto myself. I kill or I am killed.' He recognised the fabrication of specious reasoning to cloak bloodlust, but he deliberately overlooked it. He went after Cleo Rosa, to forestall eventual murder by immediate murder. Out of the room painfully, into a corridor and there she was!

She spotted him, darting away grip-launched. Her dark head twisted, left, right, left. Where to hide, even momentarily? There didn't seem to be anywhere. There was nowhere. Wherever she went, he'd follow. They both had equal reason to keep going, but she knew who had the greater stamina. She was emotionally and physically drained. Where could she hide? In desperation she thumbed the release of the nearest door. Somewhere to go. Even a second's respite. A body-shrug, a fluttering of legs and she'd gone. Her feet disappeared, kicking, and the door closed.

Derek stopped outside, resting. Musingly, he said, 'I wonder if Silver's at home?' Apparently not, or she'd be helping out the stricken Cleo Rosa by now. Cleo wouldn't be able to help herself. The slam of initial gas-shock wouldn't let her. He sang a nursery rhyme and thought a chain-thought: 'Methane, ammonia, lung-step, insalubrious for human life, choke. You've escaped me, Cleo,' he sighed, 'but you won't escape the other.' Obviously she wouldn't be going anywhere, except the longest journey of all, with a one-way ticket. Relaxed, he waited a minute or so, whistling, while Cleo Rosa died.

He thought: 'Well, I didn't kill her, did I? She just made a mistake.' It caused him disappointment rather than relief. He'd wanted to kill her. He still did. It was difficult to accept the fact that he couldn't. She was no longer alive to be killed. Anyway, what ought to be done about the body? Nothing, he decided. It would give Silver a shock, but she was tough enough to take it. Forget Cleo Rosa, then. But don't forget the power behind her!

Derek went to Communications, retrieving the poemed papers. He knew he couldn't get through to Lundren himself, so he punched digits and obtained the lowest level of government in Attica. The plate presently revealed a lowly clerk. 'Who is this? Can I help you?'

'It doesn't matter. And yes, I want a message pushing up as far as the top, to Lundren. See it reaches him; it's important.'

'This is highly irregular. I should at least have your name and...'

'It wouldn't suit you. Also I'm not parting. Tell him this: "She's dead. His hands in Thoughtworld. They're dead." Got it?'

'I think so, yes. But assuming this gibberish reaches Mr Lundren...'

'He'll understand.'

Lundren understood. His face paled as he thought of Derek's audacity; typical Merrin behaviour. He wondered what contact Lev's cousin had with Lev's spiritual descendants. Had the girl been murdered this morning according to a plan, to coincide with...? Voicelessly, the clock said, 'You have less than four hours to live!'

A pen snapped like a rifle-shot in Lundren's shaking hands. The minutes seemed to be slipping by unusually rapidly. Words took form on the wall, projected by a frightened mind: 'You've Had a Long Day, Lundren. Prepare for Night.'

Night was scheduled to arrive this morning. 'On 14-4-245, at exactly six and seven-tenths hours after dawn, the death occurred under violent circumstances of...' Joab Lundren flung aside the two pieces of the pen. He felt edgy. Surely the rebels couldn't penetrate so far? And then he amended it: surely they could! They'd already proved it. They could kill him, all right.

'Four hours,' he thought desperately. 'Less!' He had four hours in which to save himself, to hide, to escape, to survive. Meanwhile, troubles piled up in the crumbling State of New Athens.

Rebel activity right now must be frenzied. Confed ships had touched down in twelve cities. Confed authorities were following up leads, sniffing at a trail. Lundren knew the trail had an end – *his* end! If he was alive to be ended.

And Derek Merrin still lived. 'There's a circle closing in,' thought Lundren. 'I'm in the middle of it.' He couldn't do anything to halt the shrinking ring. All he could do was get out of the centre. Or could he? Wouldn't it simply be stepping out of a hot centre into a cooler one, whose heat would increase when he stumbled into it?

He didn't know. He had to chance it. If nothing else, he might be able to terminate the insufferable existence of Dizzy Derek. At any rate, it was a decision. He hoped it proved correct and thought: 'It's bound to. I won't be here when the clock tolls!' Finally he concluded that he'd no choice. Safety might not lie in Theeo, but it certainly didn't lie in Attica.

He felt better for the decision. How could it be wrong? It would save his life. That was the only criterion. It would save his life.

Chapter Eleven

He arrived unannounced, a distinguished visitor undistinguished by the usual trappings of travel and reception. For Lundren, the lift-off from Attica had been abnormally quiet and informal; an almost furtive affair, with few observers — several trusted officials, the chief officers of the ship which had brought him. It waited outside Theeo, insignificant against the powerful array of Squadron 17. The rebels should soon be attempting the life of a man who wasn't there. Lundren wished them good fortune. He made straight for Pertra and found him moodily prowling walkways. The Director was in an unused Think chamber, pensively scrutinising the walls as if they held the answers to a million questions. Lundren, clumsy in mag-boots, broke into his thought-world. 'Pertra!'

'Huh?' Startled, Pertra turned. More startled, he said, 'Lundren?'

'Prime Minister Lundren, actually,' the newcomer returned smoothly. 'One should never forget respect for those who hold one's career in their hands.' Lundren showed his hand palm-upwards, smacking a fist into it. 'A career is smashed, thus!' A sly smile appeared.

Pertra was out of patience. He thought: 'You've changed your tone, haven't you?' He remembered the spurious cordiality over the visiplate, the anxious face belying it. Now, the anxiety had gained supremacy; Lundren's attitude was proof. Craftily, Lundren changed his expression. He forced himself to relax, forcing his voice to become ingratiating. 'Well, Professor, can I be of help? You seem to have difficulties up here.'

'Nothing insurmountable. The Confed have their eyes on things.'

'Over the heads of the Thirteen? Is that advisable? Your position . . . '

'Is unimportant,' Pertra said heatedly, refusing to be threatened. 'And yes, it is advisable! Not to mention its being the correct procedure.' He returned Lundren's glare with equal firmness. 'After all, the Confed quite obviously *is* over the heads of the Thirteen! Or would you disagree?' He knew he was virtually sacrificing his Directorship, but somehow it didn't seem to matter.

'Yes, I'd disagree so far as Theeo is concerned! The Thirteen created this installation. They take the decisions regarding it.'

'In other words, I take the decisions regarding it. I am the person on the spot, Thirteen-appointed. And I decided to call in the Confed, because events of this magnitude are their responsibility, not ours . . . yours!'

'I'm glad you see the distinction, Pertra.'

'I do. I recognise the writing when it's on the wall.'

For some reason Pertra couldn't grasp, Lundren stiffened. Fear tied a painful knot in Lundren's belly. Perhaps Theeo could transpire to be every bit as perilous as Attica?

Pertra saw the fear and enjoyed it. 'Rest assured, no sabotage or attempted theft will be unpunished. The Confed have . . . ' He stopped as the door hissed open. Erranlal entered quietly, behind Lundren. 'Nice sense of drama,' thought Pertra, then resumed. 'The Confed have sent us themselves, embodied in a single . . . '

'Tuahi,' said the Tuahi. The word momentarily immobilised Lundren. His cheeks crimsoned, then coloured through pallor to a sickly grey. Fighting for control, he turned around slowly and awkwardly. His eyes widened with shock. 'Tynar!'

'Not so. Erranlal. Merely a brother. Merely, too, a representative of the Confed with absolute discretion and absolute powers.' The effort at intimidation succeeded with Lundren where it had failed with Derek. 'It occurs to me that I must uncover everything amiss in Theeo. Then, of course, act accordingly. According to my own initiative. With . . .

Erranlal paused, piercing Lundren with a sharp stare that made him wriggle, 'absolute powers!'

Gradually Lundren mastered himself, shrugging off the shock. 'I see. Our interests coincide, then. These crimes by the Empire must cease. You and I, between us, will bring it about.'

'An excellent idea! Although who mentioned the Empire, pray?' Erranlal spoke softly and carefully, baiting the other. 'The Empire?' he prompted.

'Naturally! Who else? It's common knowledge that Benlhaut does all it can to antagonise the Confed. Any fool can see it's Saril who's responsible for both the sabotage and the more serious crimes!'

'This fool can't see it.' The Tuahi smiled a very small smile, concealing a very large amusement. 'They may want Theeo, yes; I concede it. But Saril, in my estimation, is hardly warped enough to decree the theft of Theeo and its partial disablement. The former, yes, possibly. The latter, no, no.'

'Oh, nonsense!' rapped Lundren. 'I'll personally ensure that the Confed sends a strongly worded note to Benlhaut. This intolerable mistreatment of Theeo must end! I possess influence, remember. The Emperor – whether or not you can perceive his culpability – has to be warned off. Scared off, if necessary! If it needs a commencement of hostilities . . .'

'*You'll* ensure it?' Erranlal asked with dangerous calm. 'Even *I* couldn't do it. Nor would I, having retained a little sanity in my head. Have you considered the implications of full-scale war?' Lundren considered them, but they scarcely registered.

Erranlal allowed a long deliberate silence to unnerve Lundren before he spoke again. 'On the question of culpability for attempted theft, I reserve judgement. On the question of sabotage, however, I pass judgement! On you, ex-Prime Minister, on you!'

'You're out of your mind!'

'Not at all, although I suspect you are! May I disrespectfully suggest Erranlal's Hypothesis? Not so brilliant as my brother's, but much easier to verify. It reads like this: That

121

one Joab Lundren, disappointed would-be Thinker, resentful of another's renown as Father of Thoughtworld, sadly and badly overestimated his own powers and his supposed influence with Confed Central . . .'

'You're raving!'

' . . . and dreamed up a plan whereby he could appear as, shall we say, Saviour of Thoughtworld? by relying on imaginary influence in order to persuade the Confed to act on an unsubstantiated accusation against the Empire, to Thoughtworld's presumed benefit.'

Lundren laughed. It sounded off-key, harsh and forced. 'I've never heard . . .'

'Truth stated so bluntly? No, perhaps not. I further suggest that your plan is as unsound as your brain. On New Athens, you're supreme. Within the Thirteen, you're probably also supreme. But when it comes to the Confed, ex-Prime Minister, you're a silent voice yelling into ears your voice can't reach.'

'Congratulations on your imagination, Erranlal! I fancy it wouldn't stretch to imaginary evidence, would it?'

'I confess it wouldn't. Neither does it need to. Allow me to present someone.'

On cue, Derek swam in. He circled Lundren fast, like a troublesome insect. 'I've been promoted. I now hold the title of Evidence, Finger on the Trigger, although the weapon's not functioning too well now.' He came to horizontal attention by Lundren's shoulder and hurt his own forehead with a crisp sarcastic salute. Then he hurtled ceilingwards and clung on it, quiet.

'My evidence,' observed Erranlal. 'He tells an interesting tale.'

'That idiot? His word against mine?' Again Lundren laughed harshly.

'Why not? He's a Thinker; you aren't. That carries weight.'

'This carries more!' Suddenly there was a pistol in Lundren's hand. It cracked as he leaned backwards to fire up at Derek. He missed, but the bullet embarked upon the whining and unpredictable trajectory Dizzy knew only too well. Lundren's abrupt gasp proved he hadn't expected to loose random death, with odds of only three-to-one against it finding the person who'd released it. He began to fumble along the walkway towards a door, Erranlal and Pertra following, not chasing him but just trying to escape a bullet that was impartially chasing anybody. It whistled in air, clattered on steel, a murderous mote.

The door opened and Lundren stumbled through. Erranlal got out next. Pertra was a yard short of the door when the bullet stopped with a sickening sound: the squelch of ripped flesh, the crackle of snapped bone. Pertra screamed and Erranlal turned back. The Director irascibly waved off his attentions. 'My wrist, that's all. Catch that maniac. I'm okay.'

Clutching his wrist and trailing bloodmist, Pertra brought up the rear of a bizarre procession in the corridor: Lundren in the lead, shrewdly firing as he staggered, patterning the air behind him with a singing spray of potential extinction; Erranlal not far off, walkway-bound, dodging automatically although the bullet couldn't be dodged; Derek zigzagging just above floor-level, capable of catching up but sensibly holding back.

Eventually Lundren halted his grounded flight. He placed himself solidly against a wall and menaced the others with the gun. Behind them, death shrieked as though with displeasure at finding nowhere to settle. Bullets twanged, too far away now to be dangerous. Blood surrounded Pertra. Erranlal's clothes showed several lacerations. Derek was unhurt.

'Give yourself up,' the Tuahi urged. 'There's no escape and leniency might be considered. Diminished responsibility . . . ' An oath from Lundren cut off the plea. Dizzy and Pertra exchanged scared glances. Next to Lundren was a door. They knew where it led and doubtless he did, too. He'd most likely halted here deliberately, by design rather than by accident. If he went through in his demented and desperate state he could cause disaster.

They didn't realise how large a disaster until he told them. 'You know what's through here?' They nodded. 'You know that a handful of commands to those computers can blow

Theeo way out of position? A stabiliser used for purposes the exact opposite of stability?'

Pained, Pertra thought: 'He's crazy! He'd really whip us out of true, probably to fall into a star. Himself as well.' Aloud he shouted: 'Think of yourself, man! Do you want to die?'

'No, but I don't intend to live in disgrace. I believe I'd rather die than that. Taking Theeo with me, of course!' Lundren wet his lips. 'Then there's no one to sully my name. Only a terrible accident. Theeo ...'

'Swept into the heart of a star,' interrupted Pertra.

'You ignorant fool! I mean something more positive than that. Space contains plenty of emptiness; we might drift forever without getting drawn into starheart. I mean something more immediate. Something total and instant. If I give commands to the computers ...'

'You can't,' Erranlal stated calmly. 'They respond to sixteen voice patterns, no more.'

'Seventeen. You forget I was here, and influential, when Theeo was constructed.' Briefly, Lundren regretted the necessity of having to destroy the planetoid. He'd foreseen the possibility and arranged for it, but it should have been an unsuspecting Cleo Rosa, not himself, who did it. By rights, he should have been safe on New Athens, except he couldn't be safe on New Athens today. And perhaps never again.

Agony lanced Pertra's arm. 'They'll respond to you?'

'Of course! To A-block, B-block, the Director. And me. You know what happens when I speak a pre-set eleven-figure sequence into the master comp?' Apprehensive silence met him and he shattered it with a shout. 'Bang! Up she goes! The lot! Theeo and everybody in it. Vaporised, just like that!' He snapped a finger and thumb. 'A rather cunningly concealed device. Utter destruction.' He was shaking now, his voice approaching hysteria. 'Me too, but so what?'

Erranlal said, 'I don't believe you.'

'As you wish. Maybe you won't believe you're dead, but I assure you it'll make no difference. You're as good as dead now. We all are.'

'Lundren, suppose I let you free? Out of Thoughtworld, into your ship, out of the area altogether. No pursuit, I promise you. You helped to create this place; does that mean nothing? Have you no pride in it? Could you annihilate the greatest advance in centuries? I give you my pledge and that of the Confed: no pursuit, if we can have the chance to take those computers to pieces and nullify your device.'

At Erranlal's humility and desperation, Lundren smiled with genuine pleasure. 'Oh, a lovely speech! But I don't trust you. Once I'm on my way, all I'll get for my generosity is a concentrated burst of firepower from Squadron 17.'

He moved towards the door, but the gun and his eyes remained steady. 'The numbers of death,' he chuckled. 'The figures of destruction.' In the dream-haze of madness and imminent suicide, he began to giggle. The numbers squeezed out amid a stream of chilly laughter. '9–2–8–3–7–4–6–5–5–0–1. The key to Kingdom Come! The inward-facing blast whose heat detonates a crust-hidden Armageddon!'

His cachinnation rang out and Derek swooped. Pertra saw his chance, his last chance, and moved as quickly as he could, a pain-crippled boot-hobble. Erranlal was slightly more agile as he came in at the no-gun side. In air, Derek dived down, shrieking a crazy terrifying noise which temporarily disconcerted the man he had to kill. Lundren tried to cover them all at once while struggling with the door release. The pistol splashed fire twice and Pertra took both shots. He stayed erect, boot-held, swaying. He was unconscious, flesh-torn at left wrist, right shoulder and right side. A brisk glance and Erranlal thought: 'He'll live. Someone else won't.'

The gun sailed off fast, released from Lundren's grasp by an expert chop from Dizzy. It numbed the arm. A straight-fingered jab to the throat drew a choking gasp from Lundren. A fist to the jaw rattled his head back into the wall. His gaze filmed over with fading awareness and Dizzy kept going. By the time he stopped, Joab Lundren, bloody-faced but alive, had been unconscious for five minutes. Erranlal didn't interfere. Partly satisfied, Derek retrieved the gun. The touch of it flooded his mind with memories: Lev, Karl, Robert, 238, a dead nurse, bulging eyes, a kiss that was horror from a beautiful girl. Through it all, he knew exactly what he was doing. Despite it all, he knew exactly what he was going to

125

do. He clutched Lundren's collar and put the gun to his lined head. Erranlal used his absolute discretion and looked the other way. When he turned round, he asked Derek to call medical attention for Pertra. Similar treatment for Lundren would have been a superfluity. Robots came along and gently bore the Director away. Elsewhere, others were summoning qualified physicians among the Thinkers. Pertra would be taken care of. Erranlal watched more robots arrive to fetch the corpse.

'I misjudged you, Dizzy, on our first meeting. I apologise. That done, we'll bring in electronics experts from 17 out there. They should manage to get at the trouble, irrespective of our not remembering the sequence. A day or two and . . .'

'Why bother?' broke in Derek. 'It's quicker simply to locate the device, the bomb or whatever, and then have heavy tackle brought in from 17 to dig it up.' Humming, he went through the door. 'I'll see to it.'

'How?' Beset by sudden doubts, the Tuahi followed.

'Easy.' Dizzy wrapped one leg round part of the master computer, for anchorage. 'It's in the crust. We find out where. We dig. Easy.' He finished the tune he was humming, then recited, '9–2–8–3–7–4–6–5–5–0–1.'

'You remember it?'

'Obviously.' He seemed surprised that Erranlal hadn't. 'Begin with the highest single number, 9, then decrease it by one, skipping a place each time, as far as the ninth digit, 5. The second number is the lowest that'll allow you to climb upwards by one each time, alternating, and match the ninth digit, 5, with an eighth digit of 5. See? Then cap it off with the two you haven't used so far, 0 and 1. It's easy.'

'Oh,' said Erranlal faintly. 'Only how do we locate the device?'

'Easy. Like this.' Derek picked up the computer mike and to Erranlal's horror began to rapidly spit out numbers: '9–2–8–3–7–4–6–5–5–0 . . .'

'*Derek!*'

'10,' said Derek, and put the mike back. 'What's wrong?'

'Nothing, apparently.' The Tuahi looked around. Everything was fine. 'What didn't you do?' He gave a sickly grin. 'And what did you do?'

'I didn't say the final number – 1. If I had . . . ' Dizzy gestured eloquently. 'And I did locate Joab's pet. Look!' He pointed to a map on the wall, showing all Thoughtworld's external blast tubes and other surface features. A red light burned steadily. 'That's the tube I activated with the first nine digits. And that,' his finger dropped, indicating green letters below the projection, 'gives force and duration of blast; in this case, a string of noughts. No force, no duration, no blast. It's controlled by the tenth digit, the 0. A blast of force 0, for 0 seconds. That's no blast at all.'

'Very wise,' commented Erranlal drily. 'It nearly makes sense.'

'Oh, it's perfectly clear. You see, the comps won't accept a sequence with eleven numbers, except for that one specially rigged death-series conjured up by somebody who needn't concern us any more.'

'Hmmm. They won't accept eleven, save in the Lundren series? So you couldn't previously have blown yourselves up accidentally unless you'd fallen into a millions-to-one tragic error and used the special eleven?'

'Which is improbable. I mean, under what other circumstances would any of us have ordered a force-0 blast for no time flat, a nought for the tenth digit? Four numbers to select the tube; the next five to align it; the next to control the blast potency – force 1 to force 9. Never force 0.'

'I concede. Only why the 10 you spoke into the mike?'

'No reason. It could have been 10, 11, 12 or upwards. The comps only understand 0 to 9. Anything above 9 is meaningless. The 10 was appropriate, though. Thirty-two years of Thoughtworld, twenty-one Directors. Thirty-two minus twenty-one leaves eleven. Take away another one for Lundren, who's been subtracted anyway. That leaves ten. See?'

'Almost.' Erranlal decided never to try and fathom Dizzy's brain.

Derek touched the red light. 'Well, we know where the bomb is.'

'We do indeed. Under the plaque.'

*

Out on the surface, Erranlal thought angrily: 'I should have guessed!' Self-reproach scored his mind: 'I should have known, I should have seen! I was here, for God's sake! The bastard did it right under my insensitive nose!' The fact that guessing wasn't part of his cautious nature offered no mitigation. He still cursed himself for not guessing. He remembered the funeral, the service and the gathered dignitaries. He'd been present on behalf of his late brother, Tynar, Father of Thoughtworld. He remembered meeting Lundren and thought that his brain must have folded some time since 212. A few hours ago, Lundren had been shocked to see an unexpected Tuahi. Irrationally, he'd associated the sight with the dead Tynar rather than the living Erranlal.

Soundlessly, a sturdy mechanism drilled holes in Thoughtworld.

The thought of a bomb somewhere beneath his feet cooled Erranlal's flesh. It was all very well to remind himself that a heat-detonated device shouldn't explode because of vibration. The fact remained that it might.

Squadron 17 formed an unnecessary show of power, in motionless formation close by. Lundren's ship was still waiting, dwarfed, because nobody had bothered to inform the pilot about his passenger's decease.

A detail from 17 manned the drill, moving it to and fro. Shafts dotted the vicinity of the plaque, ready for excavators to stick steel tongues in and flick out rock and rubble. Among the rubbish, a deadly device ought to be lurking. Disbelief touched the Tuahi. Surely Lundren had been bluffing? After the incredulity came an inner command, to test the veracity of his claim: 'Get Derek to go and warble eleven digits!' Disbelief vanished, put to flight by an increased cooling of Erranlal's flesh. He shivered inside the suit and glanced around.

Thinkers were everywhere, watching. Those from A-block and B-block seemed filled with a gleeful excitement incompatible with the presence of a device capable of vaporising Theeo. Erranlal decided it must be because a guilt-shadow had lifted from them as he'd released the news of the saboteur's capture and execution. The survivors now knew they weren't suspects.

Characteristically, Erranlal worried about his lifeline as he watched Thoughtworlders watching the workers from 17. He also worried in case the drills sliced too deep and holed Theeo. He could only hope the drillers knew what they were doing. They ought to. He'd told them often enough.

Derek seemed the happiest Thinker of all – laughing, helping, grip-skipping like a child, as if another's death had torn a burden from his brain. Hands touching, Arkon Vitch and Silver kept up a constant intercom conversation. Occasionally their helmets touched, their eyes met. And Vitch frowned, thinking of unkissable lips. The single exception to the near-delirium of relief was Gormal, a gigantic loneliness, aloof. Withdrawn physically and mentally, he stood apart, subdued, quiet and remembering.

Erranlal wondered about the Empire. He felt safer when he stared at Squadron 17, and felt terribly insecure when he glanced at the ground. With twisted logic, he blamed himself for Lundren's having planted the device so many years ago, before the shovels sealed the tomb supposedly for all time.

Squadron 17 was a mighty metal proximity, invincible. Lundren's ship waited, a miniature uselessness. Black space stared with unwavering star-eyes.

The Tuahi ordered the diggers in. 'Take it easy. One hole at once. You've all year if you need it.' Excavators lumbered noiselessly forward. Improvised claws held them to Thoughtworld, a multiplicity of jointed legs and talons embedded deep into rock. Erranlal considered his engineers had done a quick praiseworthy job – only it wasn't finished yet. The chancy part was just starting.

Surrounding the work area, ten small gadgets held out extensible magno-grabs. Erranlal worried. 'When it comes, don't miss it. Catch it!' He realised it might be no hazard even if it escaped. It could drift innocuously forever, or explode harmlessly in starheart. Or it could get tangled up near the heat-source of an unsuspecting vessel, or tumble into a planet's gravitational field and obliterate a city. He knew the odds were long, but he still didn't like them.

Carefully, a scoop probed the first hole, slashing up tons of rubble. It dwindled towards infinity, a muck-scatter, a

9   129

rock-mess. Nobody troubled to try and stop it. Erranlal breathed slightly.

The second hole produced more debris, nothing of note. Erranlal breathed more confidently. Holes three, four and five yielded similar rubbish. The Tuahi began to feel complacent.

The plaque went spinning. One of the grab-handlers made a quick, instinctive snatch, then realised his mistake. The grab retracted. Ten grabs waited. Erranlal heard unruffled conversations and quiet comments. The spectators made him less anxious because of their own lack of anxiety.

Silver screamed when the first corpse leapt out. A mute mummy, it grimaced with bared teeth. Open eyes gazed at nobody and startled everybody. Perfectly preserved, it swam into space without strokes. Its limbs were set into fantastic attitudes, right-angled, wrong-angled, impossible in life, ghastly yet possible in death – a mortal erstwhile plasticity, rock-moulded. Several more cadavers followed, grinning hideously and then mercifully vanished. Only Dizzy Derek counted them: six. Not that it mattered. Squadron 17 hung frozen in void, a tableau of technological skill, silent and still.

Corpses eight and nine wobbled outwards into darkness, escorted by equally lifeless waste. The work area was a hole that gaped like a strangled dead mouth. Erranlal wondered whether the whole exercise was doomed to discover nothing, since nothing had been hidden. He didn't know what to think. Temptation hammered him: 'Derek and his eleven digits. You'll learn the truth then. If it doesn't kill you.'

When the tenth body was exhumed, Gormal groaned. His legs buckled, but he remained upright. Derek stared in dumb amazement at a dead face: dark, oval, black-eyed and topped by ebon hair – the features of Cleo Rosa, but arranged differently into masculinity and middle age, rearranged into death.

Dizzy felt cold and thought: 'You poor kid! What was he? grandfather, uncle? Too long ago to be your father.' The reason for *JL: An Attack!* became clear – if he made allowance for the distorted ratiocination of an off-balance brain. One of Cleo's relatives had been killed working on Thoughtworld – killed accidentally, but that might not alter the viewpoint of diseased thinking; killed at least ten years before her birth, but that might not alter anything either. And not killed personally by Lundren, although Derek could make out the cerebral pattern she must have woven. With Tynar dead, Lundren typified Theeo. Theeo had taken one of her family. Therefore, by convoluted false reasoning, Lundren had been responsible for the death.

It made a crazy sort of sense. Dizzy couldn't imagine what hold Lundren must have had on her. Enough to make her into a potential assassin. Enough to scare her into the attempts at murder. Enough to get her killed!

The last corpse came up riding a bomb. In a tangle of debris, it looped skywards on a metal case. All ten grabs lashed out magnetic hands. Magnoplates slammed into the corpse and cut it viciously. Pieces of undecayed dead flesh splashed across the void.

Derek hardly saw them. He was still watching the diminishing dot of a dark man with ebon hair. He knew he hadn't accounted for Cleo Rosa's crimes completely. Perhaps she'd worsened since arriving in Thoughtworld. Perhaps Vitch's Corollary bore a good deal of truth. An unanswerable question. The dark corpse disappeared into the unanswerable question which was the universe.

A grab whisked to within inches of the bomb and Theeo stood still. It was like the stoppage of time, or the end. It was like abrupt entropy. It stopped all sentient movement not by bodily paralysis but by psychological shock. Something had happened – something bad!

Erranlal thought: 'Tractor beam!' He looked up and saw seven ships low over Theeo. Too lethal to be doubted, the blunt snouts of scores of cannons held steady on the planetoid. They maintained a close looming threat while the beam maintained a grip Squadron 17 didn't dare break. Any missile a fraction of a degree adrift would knock Thoughtworld into early eternity. If they tried to snip the beam, the cannons would snip Thoughtworld in the same instant.

The Tuahi could sympathise with his commanders' dilemma: unidentified vessels moving in, whether or not to fire? They could be friends, they could be enemies. It was a nasty situation. Throw in the additional complication of Theeo's nearness and he couldn't blame them for just holding fire and hoping. 'Benlhaut?' he asked himself, thinking aloud.

'No.' It was Derek, beside Erranlal, surprising him. Dizzy's expression revealed strange, hurtful and inexplicable emotions. He stared in astonishment at the blacked-out markings of the seven ships. 'I recognise them. I know them. I . . . ' Then his words broke down into a muffled gasp and silence.

Erranlal said uncertainly, 'Not Benlhaut?'

'No. Rebels.'

Chapter Twelve

'Rebels?' echoed the Tuahi.

'That's right. From New Athens. Lev's successors.' Troubled, Derek recalled his last view of three of the ships: camouflaged, hidden in a jungle against the day when it might become necessary to flee the planet. He thought: 'Well, it became necessary. We just didn't get the breaks.' He could imagine the post-238 insurrectionists regrouping, growing and stealing more ships. Sadly, it seemed their ambitions had grown, too.

Above Theeo, everything hung in dread stasis: the seven rebels, the ineffectual invincibility of Squadron 17 and impartial space. On the surface, Erranlal snapped his mind into activity and sorted out his priorities. Let stalemate endure; he couldn't change it. At the moment it was vitally important to capture Lundren's device. If it escaped now, it would almost certainly find some means of detonating amongst the rebel vessels; not in itself a bad thing, but it wouldn't be too good for Thoughtworld.

He yelled into the intercom, 'Get that bomb! Forget the rest!' Incredibly, it was still within reach. Mere seconds had passed since the tractor beam first appeared, agonisingly long seconds. The nearest magno-grab jabbed for the bomb, missed and extended itself upwards after fleeing metal. It skimmed it, captured it, then another grab clashed with it. The second one snatched the device securely while the first, knocked out of control, began to rip itself loose of the rock. Claws came free and the plate-tipped arm swung wildly. Erranlal heard the machine's handler shriek in sudden panic. Eventually, somewhere out in the void, the panic would die slowly and the handler would die more slowly.

The machine lifted into emptiness on its final journey and Erranlal noticed further tragedy. A group of nearby spectators swung dead or injured on slender lifelines. He felt sickened by the awful wounds caused by the swinging arm. Then he saw the two healthy, uninjured, living people the machine had killed.

Severed lines trailed stiffly as Arkon Vitch and Silver departed in life to death. Already they were beyond the limit of the extensible grabs. They couldn't be magnetically brought back. They were so close, yet so lost.

Arkon's arms hugged Silver to him, suit to suit. Helmets met. Simultaneously, both visors slid open, opened deliberately. Erranlal couldn't understand it. Then all at once he could. Arkon Vitch kissed Silver – their first kiss and their last. Her arms clung and his arms clung. Inextricably, they tumbled upwards. Their lips also clung with desperate dying desire. Erranlal watched with dampness in his eyes as the two bodies dwindled; floating, twisting, curling, swirling, embracing, together, dead.

It was a first/last kiss that might last forever.

'What now?' thought Erranlal. There were plenty of possibilities, none of them pleasant. Squadron 17 could take a chance. Result: probable rebel losses from nought to seven, certain total loss of Theeo. The rebels could fire. Result: certain loss of seven ships, certain loss of Theeo. Again, the rebels could simply drag Thoughtworld away and defy 17 to shoot. Result: probable successful theft of Theeo, definite extinction for everyone on the surface, who would be swept off. Whichever way he looked, it looked grim.

Derek's certainty of the rectitude of rebellion was failing. By all means turn against a tyrant like Lundren. But why perpetrate such monstrous crimes as the abduction of Thoughtworld and its Thinkers? Why attack and kill? Obviously the aims had changed since Lev was in charge.

Derek glanced at the carnage and glanced at the seven ships. It hurt to connect the two, but he couldn't avoid the association. A faction with whom he'd fought in 238 was now fighting against him and against innocent Thoughtworlders. He couldn't think of any reason to bring a New Athenian problem, a local war, out into space. Involving Theeo must inevitably involve the Confed. And if the rebels thought they could beat the Confed, they'd lost touch with reality.

While Squadron 17 and the seven enemy vessels stayed immobile, frenzied work went on below, on Theeo. Corpses were being collected, cut free of lifelines and carried down the hole. Gradually the dead were being separated from the dying and the injured. Little by little, some people in the injured category would slip through into the dying. Some of the dying would slip through into the dead.

Derek looked for Gormal, but couldn't find him anywhere. He grip-walked moodily to the spot where he'd last seen him, a large quiet sorrow. Derek knew something had been shaping between Gormal and Cleo, something that couldn't be prevented by racial differences. It was dead now, because Cleo was. It couldn't shape into anything but solitary grief. He'd noted the grief in Gormal's attitude, noted the shock when the tenth body had come up out of the hole. He had more than a suspicion of what he'd find where Gormal should be, but where Gormal quite clearly wasn't. Stunned despite the expectation, he found it: an empty lifeline, not severed, simply unfastened. Of his own volition, Gormal had followed Cleo Rosa into death, followed the corpse of a dark man out into darkness, left behind the emptiness of life and chosen the emptiness of the universe.

Sadness descended on Derek; Gormal's suicide, Arkon and Silver grab-killed, Cleo killed by accident whilst rushing from murder – A-block depleted, reduced to one Thinker: himself.

Apprehensively, Erranlal watched annihilation come towards him. Stuck to a magno-plate, Lundren's bomb was lowered to the ground, lashed down to grips. He'd feel safer when experts up in 17 had rendered it harmless. It sat beside him like encased doom, tied by bonds it could burst into vapour. He didn't like it. He wished it were as dead as Lundren. Through his fear, an irony amused him: Lundren had intended to 'save' Theeo from the Empire, never realising that the threat had been from outside the Empire, from his own hated foe, no less. If he were still alive, he'd be facing old enemies on a new battleground.

'*That's enough wandering,*' the Tuahi told himself, '*more urgent matters press!*' Such as getting out of what appeared to be an insoluble predicament; such as persuading the rebels to stop being naughty and give Thoughtworld back; such as contacting 17 and telling everybody for God's sake not to do anything rash or supposedly heroic; such as thinking his way out of a mind-maze whose entrances and exits seemed to have all been blocked up.

'*Absolute powers,*' he thought despondently. It was a nice phrase, but his powers didn't feel very absolute just now. They felt negligible. He prayed for guidance but couldn't be altogether sure where he wanted guiding, except *out*! Somehow, in some fashion, by someone.

Unfortunately, everybody else would be relying on *him*! The tractor beam never relaxed. The seven ships did nothing. The fabulous armament concentration of Squadron 17 was worthless. It looked like a deadlock with no key to undo it. Erranlal thought round and round in circles, getting nowhere. Then he saw the flitter arcing down from 17. Obviously somebody, somewhere, had done something.

The inside of the rebel ship was a shambles. Erranlal contrasted it with the tidy efficiency of military vessels. These were plainly desperate creatures fighting a desperate against-the-odds action with anything they could lay their thieving hands on. Still, they had at least taken the initiative by contacting the Squadron, demanding to speak to the highest official obtainable in one of their own ships, on their own terms. They were in a strong position to demand. Erranlal was acutely conscious of his single link with 17: the flitter. It wasn't much. If the rebels took it into their heads to kidnap him, they'd very likely get away with it. And with him. And with Theeo. He knew he'd need every atom of negotiating skill he could raise. He'd have to think swiftly, talk well, concede where necessary, risk turning tough if it seemed advisable.

Faces stared at him: stern, determined, keen-eyed. No weapons were in evidence here, but he was alone with about three dozen rebels. They'd manage him bare-handed if they had to. He realised he was in a serious spot not only for himself personally, but also for Theeo, the Confed, the very concept of an authority which would tolerate no recalcitrance. The rebels stared, waiting for him to make the first move.

He pulled out papers and waved them. 'Erranlal. Confed Plenipotentiary. Tynar's brother, if that counts for anything.' Apparently it didn't. 'Now, shall we get to business?' 'Be brisk,' he thought. 'Pretend you're in control of the situation. And of yourself. Even if you're not. Be firm until the time comes to bend.' Mentally, he added a caution: 'But not too firm!' He must speak to them on equal terms, treat them as equals not as inferiors. A quick glance showed him exactly who was superior to whom at the moment.

'You're Erranlal,' said one of the rebels, a tall, scarred, red-faced human. He looked a no-nonsense type, clearly the leader. 'I've seen pictures. You're no imposter.' He gazed around at his colleagues. 'Hard but fair. A shrewd customer. He'll be okay.' The summary over, he fell silent, waiting.

The Tuahi felt awkward, vulnerable and out of his depth. It seemed he'd got to play all the opening shots, but he wasn't certain what the game was. He might make the right moves but in the wrong game. 'Well, I'm here. At your mercy, as it were. I'll grant you were sensible to initiate some form of action. We couldn't have stayed deadlocked forever. Please state your requests. Feel free to ask.'

'We're not asking,' said the red-faced man. 'We want you here to *tell* you something. To tell you what you're going to do. What the Confed's going to do.'

'To tell me? Have you the power?'

'You know damned well we have! We've got Theeo. Okay, there's a lot of opposition on the doorstep, but we've still got Theeo. Anything happens to us, Thoughtworld exits.'

'I see that,' Erranlal admitted. 'Although before you tell me what I'm going to do, how about imparting your plans? Where do you intend to take Thoughtworld?'

'Nowhere. It's fine for us exactly where it is, so long as

137

we're driving! It's our hostage; the Confed'll pay ransom. Then you can have it back. Simple.'

'Simple? You must be!' Erranlal saw the rebel's lips tighten, a quick anger that faded quickly. 'You honestly think Confed Central will dig into its pockets and set a precedent for any bunch of mercenary clowns with a few ships and a nerve? They'd sacrifice Theeo rather than . . . '

'Shut your bloody mouth! Nobody mentioned money.' To Erranlal's surprise, there was no rancour in the man's tone. He sounded genuinely upset to have been labelled wrongly. 'Some things money won't buy. Like freedom. The end of oppression. The disclosure of another side of life on Peace Planet. Most of all, the removal of that despot Lundren!'

'Lundren's dead,' Erranlal stated quietly.

'If you're trying to use lies to get out of . . . '

'I said Lundren's dead. He did need removing, I agree. He doesn't now – except in so far as he's a somewhat offensive-looking corpse.' Several low chuckles escaped – a good sign. 'A gun popped whilst being held against his forehead. He owns very little head now. In fact he's a bloody mess. If you want to remove him, help yourself. He's in Theeo; he won't run away.'

Laughter came from the background, but the spokesman didn't join in. Across his face, disbelief chased the wish to believe. The wish vanished and disbelief remained. 'Could you prove it?'

'Definitely. Send down any of your people. Go yourself. Verify what I've told you. Naturally I'll stay here, as surety. You'll discover the truth: a rather old human body, more or less terminating at the neck.'

More laughter echoed, louder. Even the leader smiled. 'We'll check.'

'Please do. You'll find Lundren every bit as dead as you could possibly hope him to be.' Erranlal paused, stretched out a shrewdly timed silence, then played his main shot. With luck, it should start the game swinging his way. 'A man called Merrin killed him.'

'*Merrin?*' It was a startled chorus.

'Merrin, yes. A close relative of *the* Merrin. A man named Derek.'

'God! Derek got through, did he? I'm glad of that. Was he hurt?'

'Not where it shows,' said Erranlal, and thought: 'Lord, he's talking to me like an old friend discussing another old friend.' Aloud, he continued: 'Would it help in any way if I had him brought up? A word or two with 17 and it's done.'

'Do it.'

Erranlal did it. 'He's coming. Now . . . ' Again he dropped a silence over the company. 'I hate to do this, but serious crimes have been committed and they can't be overlooked.' Into the silence he snapped suddenly, 'You idiots! You utter morons! You could have saved yourselves so much distress! You kill in the effort to snatch Theeo. And why? Because you want . . . '

'Justice, that's all.'

'Justice, all right. But injustice isn't the road that leads to it!'

'Sometimes it is,' insisted the rebel, and Erranlal recognised truth. 'I'm telling you, we've had it rough under Lundren; him and his secret killers. We aren't willing murderers; we're decent people trying to make a decent life for posterity on what could become a more-than-decent planet, and being forced to do it the lousy way! Desperate situations demand desperate measures.'

'I accept that. Yes, sometimes injustice is the only road. Nevertheless, murder's still murder. Expediency, even necessity, can't justify . . . '

'Oh, but it can! We reckon it like this: for every life we take in trying to capture the ear of the universe, we're saving a hundred. They're the ones who have to die to keep Lundren where he is. Was.'

'Hell,' thought Erranlal, 'in their position I'd be taking exactly the same stand.' His job hurt all of a sudden. It stabbed his conscience, and stranded him between viewpoints. 'The ear of the universe? You realise, of course, that you won't win public sympathy by acts of terrorism?'

'We're not after sympathy, just attention. The knowledge throughout the Confed that we exist. That evil exists. By what you call terrorism we want to draw attention to ourselves and point the finger at New Athens and shout, "There lies wickedness cloaked as Utopia." Perhaps I'm babbling, but you have to feel it to understand it. There aren't words.'

'I feel it,' the Tuahi said sincerely. 'I understand it.'

'I believe you do. Thanks. Anyway, that's what our aims have been: a spectacular hijack to spotlight a neglected problem. We're resolved to hold out for a high-powered Confed investigation of New Athens, its corrupt government, Lundren's unconstitutional Enforcement Agency and – well, the removal of the man himself. Only he's already gone. That's progress, eh?'

Erranlal matched the rebel's smile. 'It's a first step. Also, New Athens is being investigated at this moment. The instant I'm free to go, I promise a stiffer investigation; I'll press the right buttons and you'll have a Confed Enquiry as comprehensive as I can make it. And, not being overly modest, I'll add this: I can make the enquiry *big*!'

'I'm sure you can, but . . . ' The pain of saying what he didn't want to say, of saying what he had to say, tortured the rebel's face. 'Can we trust you?'

'Can you trust Derek?'

'Yes.'

'I think he'll vouch for me. Furthermore, I believe if you bring him up to date with everything we've said; if you tell him what I've promised; if you apprise him of how much my doing what I've promised means to Lev's type of people and Peace Planet generally; and lastly, if you set him on me with orders to kill me if I go back on things, why, if I don't push those right buttons, I'm as dead as Lundren!'

'You're straight. Although you realise we won't be releasing Theeo until things are on the move?'

'I wouldn't expect you to. But you must realise that there are certain . . . unpleasantries . . . to be gone through now? If there are discrepancies on New Athens, the Confed will get at them, yet it can't condone murder, even with what may be reasonable motives.' Erranlal gathered his energies for the sentence which could disrupt all the progress he'd made. 'You'll have to stand trial; you leaders, at least. It can't be avoided.'

'It can,' the red-faced man said bluntly. He'd recognised truth, too.

'Hold it!' Another rebel came forward. 'We're being dealt with fairly. Our hands aren't clean. Dirt means washing.'

Erranlal felt the bitter thrill of imminent victory. 'Thank you.' He'd almost won and he was almost sorry for it. 'I don't say murder's a good thing, but there are definitely circumstances here which could conduce to leniency. Also anything shady on New Athens is positive to count in your favour. I can't take you by force; I'm the entire strength of the Confed, but I can't take you if you don't want to come. And believe me, I appreciate your not wanting to come. Only . . .'

'Sacrifice,' the second speaker muttered. 'We were prepared to die to beat Lundren. Well, the bastard's dead, but we haven't beaten him yet. So we must smash all the filth he's left. By showing courage? I don't know. At any rate, by giving ourselves up. Letting the whole bloody universe see we aren't afraid to stand by our beliefs and what they forced us into doing. If we weren't scared of an EA chattergun, why fear a court? If we were ready to give up a lifetime, why be scared to risk part of it? Hiding on Lundren's world was imprisonment of sorts.'

The rebel leader looked pensive, watching a number of his colleagues grouping around the one who'd spoken. 'The leaders, you said? I suppose that's how it should be. Although these seven ships stay here, adequately crewed by the not-so-guilty, if there are degrees in this thing.' With an effort, he managed to grin. 'And the beam stops locked on Theeo. Not that I don't trust you, but . . . ' He shrugged, 'insurance.'

'I'd insist on it myself,' said Erranlal. 'Insurance.'

'Right, then! Sacrifice. That's what it's all about.'

'Yes, I believe it possibly is,' Erranlal said with sympathy.

Pertra lay webbed uncomfortably in his cocoon. His left arm stuck out at a right-angle. Analgesic spray spurted in a regular pulse inside the sheath covering his arm and deadening the pain that informed him he was alive. Dressings were pressed against the throbbing at his right shoulder and side.

For want of something to do, he was thinking. Mental

clarity came much easier here in Theeo, even for an untrained non-Thinker. He decided he'd done his job adequately during his short term in office. With Lundren gone, the Thirteen might be less inflexible. Perhaps his tenure wouldn't be terminated so abruptly, after all. He knew his true future was in Theeo.

Despite the strange situation, there was still a lot to do. For a start, somebody must definitely follow up the Corollary, Arkon Vitch's extension of Tynar's Hypothesis. If the Corollary were correct, as all the evidence indicated, safeguards would be needed. Sick brains couldn't be allowed to increase in misdirected potency, or Theeo's unique intellect-expanding conditions might be used for grim purposes rather than beneficial.

Pertra thought: 'Lords of Void, what if Lundren had made it as a Thinker?' It didn't bear thinking about, but he exercised his sense of communal responsibility and thought about it until he'd concluded that the Thirteen must be persuaded to tighten up their processing of aspirant Thought-worlders. He explored the Corollary thoroughly and discovered he could formulate further corollaries, theories, offshoots and ideas. An experiment with possible far-reaching consequences suggested itself: ship out to Theeo a load of so-called freaks, the people with bizarre gifts, the abnormal, the unusual – clairvoyants, telepathists, faith-healers, telekineticists, and so on.

The latter classification seemed to bear potential beyond the scope of his mind. Scour the universe for those who could manipulate matter without physical touch. Let their incomprehensible gifts grow more fantastic by introducing them to a long period of no-grav. What was to stop them moving ever larger objects, ever farther?

Suddenly, the limit was infinity. They could put Theeo into the Void Regions, instantaneously! Infinity might not be the limit, even though it wasn't a limit at all. Infinity is only a word. We don't even know what it means. All we know is what we've made it mean. And we've been wrong before!' Shocked at the implications of his cerebration, Pertra began to wonder what lay beyond infinity – a question which was manifestly absurd, contradictory and paradoxical

142

by current standards. Which meant current standards had better be modified! And fast!

Lesser possibilities hit him in an amazing flood. Let the artists come to Theeo to increase the magic and magnificence of their creations beyond imagination. Let people with marvellous imaginations come to Theeo, to imagine future things beyond modern imagination. Let the talented inventors come. In fact, let everybody come who possessed a healthy mind – to dream, to wonder, to speculate, to juggle transcendent unrestrained ideas, to cast out unwanted mind-murmurs, to exorcise cerebral sensory-screams. In short, to Think!

Pertra felt sleep lowering a soothing peace over him. He wasn't uncomfortable any more. The pain had gone, swirled up and momentarily thrown away by the brain-energy he'd burned. His outer vision closed, but his inner vision kept seeing sights of incredible wonder. The possibilities seemed endless. The endless universe beckoned with an infinity of staggering possibilities. Cosmic mystery appeared as a closed book which was gradually opening. Pertra floated into slumber with a stupendous knowledge: properly managed, Thoughtworld should be the path to a glorious future.

'And then there was one,' mused Derek dejectedly. He was A-block, all by himself. It seemed very large, very empty and very lonely. There'd be no more booming humour or poetry from huge faithful Gormal, gone now on a self-willed voyage to prove the ultimate in loyalty.

Cleo Rosa's beautiful face would never again radiate the dark splendour Lundren's evil errands had failed to erase. No one could ever bask in the alien loveliness of Silver, the scaly glitter, the iridescent hair, the twin gems of her eyes. Communications would have to get along without stalwart Arkon, who'd communicated his unquestioned love for Silver in a suicidal unquestioning lip-passion that could take them both together on the eternal ride towards eternity.

Derek missed them all: Gormal, Silver, Arkon, and, surprisingly, more than anyone else, Cleo Rosa. He couldn't understand it, but it wouldn't be denied. 'Sorry, God, you'll just have to wait.' Where was the point of The Breakthrough now? Where were the Thinkers who'd been working on it? 'Dead, dead, dead!' thought Derek bitterly – except for one, who, by murder, had in his own eyes vindicated his existence. From now on, it would be a lonely existence.

He couldn't be bothered to project his mind towards possible Breakthrough. 'Where's the reason? When we've attained the ultimate, where do we go from there?' The continued unreachable nature of the ultimate justified Thoughtworld's continued operation – at least on a non-political and higher level. When sentience reached the end of the road, it would have no choice but to stop. That seemed an ideal reason not to be in too big a hurry to reach it. Perhaps.

In an agony of solitude, Dizzy made a scene of summer: gay leaves, blue sky and bright flowers. He hovered in mid-air. Then he suddenly tired of it, wearied of it and saw its futility. It annoyed him.

Above Theeo, seven rebel ships aimed cannons against the necessity of a vengeful last-gasp cannonade. The tractor beam didn't waver. Squadron 17 guarded nothing, in nothing, from nothing. There was uneasy balance.

Inside Thoughtworld, Dizzy Derek changed summer into winter.